TH

KIDNAPPED

Bride

Bridgewater Ménage Series - Book 1

By Vanessa Vale

Cover Design: RomCon - www.romcon.com

Cover Photos: Bigstock- Lenor; Period Images

Emma James felt secure in her life. Money, social standing and the protection of her step-brother. Or so she thought. When she discovers his dark secrets, he turns on her and sells her to a western brothel to keep her quiet. There, she's forced to work or participate in an auction. A virgin auction...and she's the prize.

One look at Emma James and Whitmore Kane and Ian Stewart know she would belong to them. Marriage was the only way to truly claim her...so they bid and bid well. As their bride, they return to the Bridgewater Ranch and teach her the ways to please not one husband, but two. But danger has tracked Ian around the world and threatens their newfound relationship. Together, can they fight the demons of the past while forging a future?

This is the first book in the Bridgewater Ménage Series, where you'll meet all of the men in Kane and Ian's army regiment and discover their unusual beliefs on marriage. Read the entire series to follow along as the men, two or three at a time, claim their brides. Bridgewater: Where ménage meets marriage.

THEIR KIDNAPPED BRIDE

CHAPTER ONE

EMMA

"You may do with her as you wish. I wash my hands of her."

These were the words that I first comprehended as I awoke, my mind unusually foggy. Everything that came before was garbled as if I had cotton stuffed in my ears. My eyes felt as if lead weights were pressed upon them, too heavy to open, and a bitter taste coated my tongue. My head thumped in time with my beating heart. I didn't want to surface from the safe warmth of my slumber.

"Surely she could be spoken for easily enough. A hasty marriage. Her face and body are more than appealing to any man." A woman responded to the man's insistent words.

"No," his tone was emphatic, sharp. "That will not suffice. My money, if you please."

My head was clearing enough to recognize the voice. It was my step-brother, Thomas. Who was he speaking with, and why? The topic was odd. Everything was odd. Why were they talking in my bedroom while I slept? It was time to discern the answer.

Stirring, I pushed up from the bed to sit, my eyes fluttering open, then widening in surprise. This wasn't my bedroom! The walls were not robin's egg blue, but a garish ruby red. The room was gaudy and softly lit, equally red velvet drapes hung at the windows. The room imbued decadence, extravagance. Tawdry deeds. I rubbed at my sleepy eyes, making sure I was not dreaming, taking a moment to clear my head.

Thomas stood tall with his erect bearing by the door, palm out, speaking with a woman over a foot shorter. She wore an emerald green satin gown that had her ample cleavage all but spilling over the top and showcased a narrow waist. Her jet black hair was piled high, creatively so, in the latest of styles with artful curls down her nape. She was beautiful, her skin an alabaster white, her lips tinged with coloring, her eyes darkened with kohl. She was as decadent as her surroundings.

She moved gracefully to a large desk, situated before an unlit fireplace and smoothly opened the top drawer. Her eyes shifted to me and made notice that I was awake, but made no mention of it. She removed a small stack of bills and handed them to Thomas. He was a big man, broad and imposing, and could easily make the strongest of men nervous. But not this woman. She didn't cower. She didn't simper. She only tilted her chin up in a haughty way at the transaction.

"Thomas." My voice came out scratchy and I cleared my throat. "Thomas," I repeated. "What is happening?"

His dark eyes narrowed as he fixed his gaze on me. Only hatred showed in their inky depths. It had been disinterest that was usually there, this anger was new. His father married my mother when I was five and Thomas fifteen, both parents widowed years prior. The union was more for money than affection and when they died – he of a fall from a horse and she a year later of consumption – I was left under the guardianship of Thomas. Although he had never been affectionate or overly interested in me, I had wanted for nothing.

"You are awake," he grumbled, his mouth turned down in a frown. "The laudanum dose was not as substantial as I expected."

My mouth fell open. Laudanum? It was no wonder I struggled to comprehend. "What – I don't understand." I ran my hand over my hair, my severe bun having lost several of its pins and some long tendrils brushed along my neck. Licking my dry lips, I glanced between the strange woman and my Thomas.

My step-brother was an attractive man, in a conservative, severe fashion. He was precise, concise and exacting. Strict would also be apt, as would severe. His suit was black, his dark hair slicked and shiny with pomade, his mustache full, yet fiercely maintained. Some said we looked similarly, even though we were not formally related, our eyes the same bright blue, hair dark as night, however our countenance was quite different. Thomas's emotions matched his attire: austere and tense, a trait also found in his father. I, however, was considered to be more placid, the peacemaker in the family. With our parents dead, I lived with Thomas and his wife, Mary, and their three children. A part of a hectic household, I was always able to maintain some semblance of lightheartedness in contrast to my sibling's less generous nature.

Thomas sighed, as if wasting time on a recalcitrant child. "This is Mrs. Pratt. I relinquish my guardianship of you to her."

Mrs. Pratt did not look like any married woman that I'd ever known. None I knew of wore a dress in such a color, sheen of fabric, or daring cut. Her expression remained neutral, as if she did not wish to be involved in this conversation.

"I don't need a guardian, Thomas." I shifted to swing my legs over the side of the chaise on which I'd been sleeping. Not sleeping, drugged. The piece of furniture was an odd feature in what I surmised was Mrs. Pratt's office. This was not a topic of conversation to have lying down and I felt at a complete disadvantage. I straightened my dress and tried to tidy myself, but there was not much I could do without a mirror and a comb. "If you feel the house is too crowded, I can certainly find a home of my own. I am not without means."

Our father had been the owner of a gold mine on the outskirts of Virginia City and money had, for a time, poured in. With well placed investments, our family wanted for nothing. Every extravagance was brought in by railroad, even to such a remote and small town in Montana. This fortune had even helped fund Thomas's position in the town's government. His interest in politics, and a future in Washington, called for the well placed spending of these funds.

"No. Your money is gone." He glanced down at the nails on one hand.

I stood at his words, stunned. The room spun for a moment and I grabbed hold of the chaise for support. The money was gone? The account was ample for anything I could ever need. "Gone? How?"

He shrugged negligibly, flicking his gaze to mine for the briefest of moments. "I took it."

"You can't take my money." My eyes widened, my stomach flipped, as much from the sour effects of the opiate laced drug as to my brother's words and banal tone.

"I can and I have. As your guardian, it is within my rights to manage your funds. The bank cannot stop me."

"Why?" I asked, incredulous. He knew I was not asking after the bank, but his claim on my inheritance.

Mrs. Pratt just stood and listened, her hands clasped together at her waist. It seemed I had no champion.

"You witnessed something you shouldn't have. I need you gone."

"Wit–" I shut my mouth after I realized his insinuation. I *had* seen something I shouldn't. The other morning, Mary and I had taken the children to school before joining the women's auxiliary to discuss the plans for the summer town picnic. One of the children had forgotten their lunch pail and I volunteered to return to the house and retrieve it while Mary continued on to the meeting. Tedious as those functions were, I was thankful for a reprieve from the matchmaking older women. At twenty-two, my unmarried state was their pet project. It was their goal to see me wed before my next birthday. I, on the other hand, was not in such a rush, especially based on the supercilious and unappealing men who were under consideration.

Instead of finding Cook in the kitchen, I found Clara, the upstairs maid, lying upon the kitchen table. Her gray uniform was bunched up about her waist, her white cotton drawers dangling from one ankle as Allen, Thomas's personal secretary, stood between her spread thighs. His pants had been open to expose his manhood, which he thrust into Clara with vigor. I remained quiet and hidden in the doorway, the couple unaware of my presence, and watched their carnal actions. I knew of what happened between a man and woman in general terms, but had never seen it firsthand, and nothing like this. Not on a kitchen table!

From what my mother had told me before she'd died it was

done at night, in the dark, with only a minimal amount – and then only what was required – of skin exposed. By the intensity and vigor of Allen's motions, I thought Clara would complain or be in pain, but the look on her face, the way she tossed her head back and thrashed upon the wood surface had me thinking otherwise. He was pleasuring her. *She liked it!* Mother had said it was something to be endured, but Clara proved her statement false. The look of ecstasy upon her face could not be feigned.

I'd felt a tingling between my legs at the idea of a man filling me in such a way, making me lost to everything but what he was doing. When Clara ran her hand over her covered breasts, my nipples had tightened, ached to be touched. She hadn't just been enjoying Allen's attentions. The way she arched her back and screamed, she'd *loved* it. I wanted to feel as she did. I wanted to scream in pleasure. I was aroused by the idea of being handled thusly by a man. Unfamiliar wetness had seeped from my woman's core and I'd reached down to run my hand over the swollen flesh, even through the thick fabric of my dress. When I felt an unfamiliar jolt of pleasure from the motion, I removed my hand in stunned surprise. If my touch alone had felt so heavenly, what would it feel like being taken care of by a virile man?

Allen had thrust a few more times, and then stiffened, groaning as if injured. When he pulled his plum colored member, glistening and wet, from Clara's body, I saw not only her womanly folds, but copious white cream as well. He'd placed her feet on the very edge of the table so she was exposed and vulnerable, however the young woman didn't seem to care, either too well pleasured to bother with modesty, or she had none.

I'd licked my lips at the sight of her wantonness, her sated body replete and well used. *I* wanted to feel that way and I wanted a man to do it. Not Allen, but a man that would be mine.

My desire had been quickly doused when Thomas, previously hidden from view, came to take Allen's place between Clara's thighs. Leaning forward, he grabbed the front of her bodice and ripped, buttons skittering across the room. He lowered his head to her exposed nipples and suckled on one, then the other. I had no idea a man would do such a thing.

His hands had moved to the button on his pants and pulled his own member free. It was bigger than Allen's, longer, and wetness seeped from the tip. The secretary stood to the side, his pants set back to rights and watched, arms over his chest. Thomas lined himself up and shifted his hips so that he thrust deep into Clara's body. The woman's back arched off the table as Thomas filled her, her moan of pleasure filling the room.

I must have made a sound, a gasp, some noise that was different than the woman with whom he was fornicating because he turned his head and saw me peeking around the doorway. Instead of stopping, he pumped into her even harder, the woman's head thrashing about on the hard surface.

"Watch, I don't mind," Thomas told me, grinning, placing his palms on the table to go even deeper. "In fact, I might like knowing a virgin is learning something."

At his words I'd fled, the lunch pail forgotten.

That had been a few days ago and I'd barely seen Thomas since, out of sheer avoidance on my part. I didn't know what to say to him, nor how I could even look him in the eye knowing he not only took women with his secretary, but had broken his marriage vows. Did Mary know of his indiscretions, for I could only assume this wasn't his first. The duo seemed to be comfortable in their endeavors in a way that indicated long term familiarity. I'd readily distanced myself from Clara and Allen as well.

"I see you know to what I speak. I can't have you blathering about what you saw to the entire town. Besides, your voyeuristic tendencies are not normal for a woman of your station. I can't rightly marry you off to a friend of mine with such indecent proclivities."

He hissed the last words as if I was the one who'd been involved in those base sexual acts instead of him. I was being accused of indecent proclivities? He was the one who had careless disregard for his wife!

"Voyeurism? I wouldn't have watched if I'd known. It was the kitchen mid-morning. Thomas, I'd never–"

He sliced a hand through the air, cutting off my words. "It is irrelevant anyway. Having you about is not a risk I can take with my career. One utterance of impropriety and my chances for Washington are dashed."

"Men have mistresses, Thomas. It would come as no surprise," I countered. "Surely, Mary must know."

He laughed coldly. "Mary? I'm not worried about my *wife* and what she thinks. She would not speak ill of me. I am within my rights to ensure that."

I cringed at the thought of how he ensured her silence. Mary was a meek woman and I was coming to discover why. Mary had no grounds to protest or complain about a husband's peccadillo. A wife was completely at the mercy of her husband.

"Surely you're worried that Allen or Clara would tell tales as well." I wasn't the only one who could reveal his extramarital tendencies.

Thomas rolled his eyes. "Please, Clara was easily dispensable and Allen knows his place. He's just as driven as I am to be in Washington."

I could only imagine how he'd *dispensed* of Clara if turning me over to Mrs. Pratt was how he dealt with a member of his own family. I began to wring my hands. Thomas seemed as serious about this as everything else, removing any problem or impediment from his way with ruthless precision. It appeared he was taking care of me in just such a fashion.

I did not have to stay here and listen to him. I walked

toward the door to leave, but he held up a hand. "You have no money, no connections. Only the clothes upon your back."

I shook my head in doubt. "This is insanity, Thomas!" I waved my hands in the air, frustrated. "I have friends, a sister-in-law, neighbors! I have Father's money! I can just walk out that door and see someone on the street I know and they will help me."

"Besides your lack of money, we're not in Helena."

My arms fell to my side. My stomach plummeted. "What? You can't. I'm of age."

"True, but your father's will stated I maintained control until you reach the age of twenty-five or upon your marriage. Since you have yet to wed, I can do what I wish with the money."

"You've turned all my suitors away!" I cried out, realizing right then and there his master plan. "You've planned this all."

He smiled, albeit coldly. "We are in Simms, in Mrs. Pratt's establishment. If you walk out that door, you will be on the streets of a strange town with no one to vouch for you, with no alternative but to return to her to survive. Besides, I doubt she would let you leave. Isn't that right, Mrs. Pratt?" He didn't wait for the woman to answer. "She has paid me a tidy sum for you and I have no doubt you will need to earn your keep on your back." He sniffed. "The way you seemed to enjoy Clara's sexual awakening, I trust this will be a perfect fit for you." He eyed me from head to toe, then turned his attention to Mrs. Pratt. "Thank you for your business."

"Mr. James," she replied with a small head nod, holding the door open for him. She was going to let him go?

Thomas left, his void as big as the emptiness of my emotions. I'd been sold to a brothel! The very idea was ludicrous, unimaginable, yet here I was. Tears filled my eyes.

"It's not all that bad, Miss James. You're no longer under that odious man's thumb." She pursed her lips as she shut the door behind him. It was as if life as I'd known it had ended, the door closed on it, a new one beginning. That was what was most fearful. What did my new life entail? Would I have to service men like Clara had Allen, or would I have to suffer beneath the cruel hands of a man such as Thomas? This was insanity!

I wiped frantically at my wet cheeks. "Little consolation," I replied, looking down at the decadent Oriental rug. "The alternative, the way Thomas painted it, is not appealing either."

"That man, your step-brother, *sold* you to me." She pointed toward the closed door. "He is not a man worthy of our attentions. I say good riddance." Her soft voice held a note of iron as she waved her hand through the air with finality.

"Then why did you accept his business? Why did you *buy* me?"

Her skirts swished as she crossed the room. "To make money, of course. Yet I have a soft spot for women whose lives have become endangered. Trust me, you are better off here with me than to linger another night beneath that man's roof."

I tilted up my chin, not as confident in my situation as she. "I suspect it is dependent on what you wish to do with me."

"You are a virgin," she stated.

I blushed furiously, my cheeks hot.

"Yes, I can see by your reaction to that word alone that you are," she replied, going over to her desk, sitting down at the chair beside it. Her back was straight and she adjusted her full skirts. She might be a Madame, but she had the mannerisms of a lady.

I looked down at the pale blue morning dress I'd donned just this morning. I thought back, realizing Thomas must have laced my coffee with the laudanum. I took it black, so the bitter taste would have been well masked. The last I remember was eating a piece of toast with marmalade in the dining room.

"I suppose virginity is quite a commodity in your line of work. You are a Madame, are you not?" I countered, wanting to confirm her profession. I doubted she arranged for governesses.

She nodded once. "I am. Unlike your Mr. James, I offer you two choices."

I arched a brow as I waited to hear them. My options, which I doubted were going to be to my liking, might be better heard sitting down, so I returned to sit at the end of the velvet covered chaise on which I awoke.

"You may work here to pay off your debt. As you are innocent, you will be quite popular, I assure you. You are also quite lovely, which will make your long-term appeal guaranteed. This is the finest brothel between Kansas City and San Francisco and we cater to more *unusual* requests. The other girls will teach you all that you need to know above and beyond basic fucking with regards to meeting the men's needs."

My mouth fell open at her base language, but I supposed it was relevant to her profession and part of her everyday conversation.

I glanced down at my hands in my lap trying to collect my thoughts. A dull throb filled my head, the lingering after effects of Thomas's deviousness, it made clear thinking difficult. "And...the other choice?"

"You can pay off your debt in one evening. Tonight, in fact."

This sounded appealing, but I knew there would be a high personal price. She might be selling carnal pleasures, but this was all business.

"Oh?" I queried, very nervous about what she would say.

"A marriage auction."

I paused and stared at Mrs. Pratt. Did she say marriage and auction together? As in I would be auctioned off to a potential groom?

"I beg your pardon?" I replied, confused.

Mrs. Pratt smiled softly. "I know of several men who are seeking a wife who can handle their more intense sexual natures and dominant personalities."

I frowned. I most certainly couldn't meet those requirements. "As you've said yourself, I am a virgin. I don't know anything about...intense sexual natures."

"Good." She gave a decisive head nod. "I didn't say you needed to *know* anything about that, but that you could *handle* it."

I frowned. "There's a difference?"

"Vastly." I waited for her to clarify, but she remained silent.

"How are you so sure I can *handle* these...expectations?"

"From what Mr. James mentioned, you were aroused by the sight of a woman being fucked. Is this an accurate statement?"

I tried my best not to squirm. To admit I'd been aroused by witnessing Clara's pleasure would mean I was just like any of Mrs. Pratt's girls. It meant I truly was a voyeur, a whore even. Perhaps I did belong in a brothel.

"Well?" Mrs. Pratt asked.

"The woman was pleasured by both men. I had no idea such things were possible."

Her eyes widened slightly. "There were two men then? And

you were aroused as you watched this? Interesting." When I remained silent, afraid to let any more secrets slip, she continued. "So you *were* aroused?" She'd twisted my words around to fit her needs. "Come, Miss James, there's no need to fear speaking your feelings with me. I am a Madame. I've seen and heard it all. Nothing you, a virgin, could admit would shock me."

I couldn't voice the words, but nodded.

"Did you like watching?"

I nodded again. "I liked seeing the first man and the woman. I could have done without watching my stepbrother engaged in such activities."

"Wished it had been you that was being fucked?"

I met her clear gaze. Held it. "Yes," I whispered.

She stood, the satin sheen of her dress catching the light. "What choice do you make? Work here or marry the highest bidder?" Her blue eyes watched me. Waited.

Her words made my life seem so negligible, as if the choice were easy. I'd only woken up to this situation only minutes ago, my head still pounded from the after effects. I was now to choose my fate? "I will not marry myself to a man such as Thomas." I clenched my hands in my lap. "A multitude of men using my body is nothing in comparison to a lifetime of dishonesty, indifference and infidelity. It would be a prison without any means of escape. You met him. To suggest a permanent arrangement with the likes of him would make you of the same ilk."

A hint of emotion shown in the woman's eye. Admiration? Surprise? I couldn't be sure. "I would never marry a woman to a man who was anything but generous and caring. I am stringent in the men to whom I serve, yet protective of the women I provide. Remember, being dominant in the bedroom is quite the opposite of being cruel."

I didn't know what she meant by the last. "Why marriage? Why not just sell my virginity?"

"You would gain nothing after the first man breaching your maidenhead. You would be tarnished and your value would be that of every other girl in my employ. You would then be unmarriageable and your fate sealed. Marriage will maintain your respectability. I don't stand for men who only take from women and give nothing in return. Or you may remain here and work to earn your keep."

I had no interest in becoming a prostitute, the idea made me want to vomit, but I could only accept the woman's reassurance that I would not be shackled to a man such as Thomas on blind faith. Her oddly placed values – the need to marry me off to make money all the while maintaining my virtue – was an odd twist on my scenario and painted her in a slightly different light.

"I can imagine the life of a wife readily enough. Perhaps you can describe my other choice."

Her lip quirked up at my request. "Most girls work from six at night until six in the morning, servicing as many as twenty men. You'll soon discover your best skills and be known for them. At first, of course, it will be your innocence, but once that fades, you'll have to decide." She shrugged negligently. "Some go for straight fucking, others are known for their cock sucking. A few enjoy being fucked in the ass. Then there's being tied up, role playing, ménage, the list is quite long really."

I held up my hand, not able to keep up with her long list of services. In fact, I was still considering twenty men a night. Clearly she was forcing my hand toward marriage. That, most likely, was her intention all along, allowing me to believe I had a choice. Licking my lips, I asked the relevant question. "How much money did you pay Thomas for me?"

"Seven hundred dollars."

My brows went up. That amount of money was a drop in the bucket for the James family and I could have paid her readily enough after a quick trip to the bank, although not any longer.

"At less than a dollar a roll, that would be hundreds of men. You'll most assuredly be here for a lengthy duration. After that...." She shrugged her shoulders and let what she didn't say speak for itself. "Or you could be gone tonight."

I pursed my lips. She, in a perverse and roundabout sort of way, was helping me. She couldn't just let me leave; too much money was at stake. Marriage helped me while she helped herself. There really wasn't much choice. The groom himself wasn't a choice either. It seemed Mrs. Pratt would decide that, or at least narrow the choices to a small cadre of eligible men who had the means to offer her the money she wanted. Based on her profession and business sense, their initial requirements included baser sexual needs and wealth. "You can guarantee the man I marry is not a drunk, geriatric or a beater?"

Her blue eyes met mine. "I can."

"I'll...um...I'll take the marriage auction."

"A wise choice." She moved and opened the door. "As I said, these men want you to fulfill very distinct, very clear needs. Being dominant is not akin to being cruel. Remembering that will serve you well."

CHAPTER TWO

EMMA

Hours later, I stood before a group of men in just my shift, the new one I'd purchased with such eagerness earlier in the week. Mrs. Pratt, while seemingly kind, felt it prudent to let the bidders see more of me than what my dress exposed. Now, I was berating the very feature I'd so admired, as the material was so fine as to be translucent. I couldn't look at any of the men, seeing the looks on their faces as they looked at my body as if inspecting a horse for purchase. I kept my focus lowered to the floor.

Looking down, it prompted me to what they could see of me. The color of my nipples was plainly visible, the tight tips poking out. My shift fell to the middle of my thighs and I was sure the dark color of the hair between my legs was clearly discernible. The fine embroidery detail along the hem only drew the men's eyes to the short length. It had been pleasurable to me to wear such decadence beneath my modest dresses, with secret knowledge of what was beneath, but to be exposed in such a way to a roomful of men was mortifying. Humiliating. Downright scary.

It was almost impossible not to cover myself with my arms, to tug on the hem with trembling fingers, but Mrs. Pratt had made it clear that my future husband wanted a good glimpse of what he would purchase. If this were the case, I should be naked, however I most certainly wasn't going to suggest such an idea. Fortunately, the small room wasn't overly bright, only lit by a few lamps, which cast a muted yellow glow. It wasn't cold, but goose flesh rose on my arms nonetheless. The slight odor of kerosene combined with tobacco filled the air.

And so I stood, hands by my side, fingertips rubbing together, eyes averted from all of the men as murmurs filled the air. Mrs. Pratt was the only other person in the room and I knew all eyes were on me, the men sitting in chairs in a semicircle around me. They could have any woman below stairs, so why me? Why an inexperienced virgin when a veritable courtesan could meet their every need without the burden of wedlock? Clearly, with that option available and not taken, these men were serious about their intentions. I'd briefly glimpsed four men as I entered, but refused to meet any of their eyes. It wasn't as if I was afraid I'd be an acquaintance of any of the men – the chances were remarkably slim being in Simms, and not Helena – but I didn't want to see their looks as they took in my *dishabillé*. I didn't want to see their expressions as they gazed upon me.

"She is a virgin?" a man asked to my right.

Mrs. Pratt, who stood behind me, spoke, her words clipped and surprisingly sharp. "Do not question the integrity of my auctions, Mr. Pierce."

The man made a sound in his throat of dissatisfaction, but

did not reply.

"I want her naked," another man added.

"Emma," Mrs. Pratt addressed me instead of responding to the request. "What has a man seen of your body?"

I turned my head toward her voice, looked up at her through lowered lashes. "Ma'am?" I asked, my voice barely above a whisper.

"Has a man ever seen your ankles?"

I flushed hotly at the very idea. "No." I dropped my gaze and concentrated on the carpet beneath my feet.

"A wrist?"

I shook my head. "No."

"This is the first time a man has seen you in just a shift?"

Why did she have to point out the extent of my innocence? I took a deep breath to calm my racing heart. It felt as if it would beat right out of my chest. Licking my lips, I responded. "Yes, ma'am."

"Then, Mr. Rivers, to witness her reaction to being naked with a man will be saved solely for her husband. Bid the highest and that man will be you."

A voice spoke from my left. "She has been trained to meet her husband's needs?"

"Of course not, Mr. Potter. Her training is her husband's

responsibility."

"And pleasure." This man's voice came from directly in front of me. It was deep in timbre, rough, yet assured. I saw only his feet and lower legs. Leather boots, black pants. I refused to look higher. Pleasure, he'd said? This man would find pleasure in training me to meet his needs? A vision of Clara, her legs spread wide and being pleasured by Allen, came to mind. Had the maid been doing what the man wanted?

"Precisely," Mrs. Pratt added, her words returning me to the present. "Shall we begin? The bidding starts at one thousand dollars."

The price made me gasp. That much? No wonder Mrs. Pratt wanted to sell me to the highest bidder. She easily recouped her losses and would make a tidy profit.

The price climbed readily enough. I didn't dare to look up and see who bid. The weight of the situation was not lost on me. These voices were of men who wanted to marry me. *Marry.* And they were willing to offer a small fortune to do so. There were no courtship, no dinners, walks, or chaperoned outings. No whispered confidences, flirty smiles, stolen kisses. The men were bidding on me because of my purity, my looks and Mrs. Pratt's assurance that I would meet their sexual needs. I ran my fingers over my shift at my sides as I continued to study the paisley pattern in the carpet, willing my breath to even. This was stripping my ideals of marrying for love and replacing them with something seedy, something tawdry.

"Sold!" Mrs. Pratt said with finality, making me jump. It was over? It had happened so quickly, perhaps only a minute or two, yet my life had changed irrevocably. I was too frightened to look up and see the man who'd bid the highest. In fact, I wasn't sure who had won. Seeing his face would make it all the more real. "Mr. Kane, Mr. Monroe, congratulations. Please follow me. The doctor and Justice Of The Peace are waiting in my office."

Did she mention two men? That couldn't be. The woman took my arm and led me from the room. As we walked down the hallway I noticed the man with the boots and dark pants following. He was Mr. Kane? He was to be my husband? When we turned a corner I observed a second man following a little further behind. It was all so overwhelming, confusing. Quick. It seemed we were to wed immediately. Mrs. Pratt was a shrewd businesswoman and most certainly didn't want any chance of this man, Mr. Kane, backing out of the arrangement. Most assuredly wedding vows would see to that.

The Justice Of The Peace was a short, rotund man with a thin mustache. He had more hair above his lip than on his head. Bible in hand, he stood at our appearance. So did the doctor, or so I assumed. He was tall and trim, lanky in build, yet attractive in his dark suit. I glanced past the man with dark pants and boots, afraid that if I looked at him, all this would become real. The man who followed moved to stand unassuming in the corner. His clothes were less formal; dark pants, white shirt. His hair was longer than *de rigeur* and his skin was tanned as if he spent ample time outdoors. The color of his hair reminded me of a wheat field, where the locks were lightened by the summer sun. With his piercing green eyes focused directly on me, I felt exposed, a reminder I wore solely my shift. It was as if he could see through the fabric to my untouched skin. When his gaze held mine, I felt he could see into me, to read my very thoughts. I couldn't help but cross my arms over my chest in an attempt at modesty.

I felt my cheeks heat, my nipples tighten at the knowledge he was looking me over. When I glimpsed, from my periphery, the corner of his mouth tilting up, I knew he would not be my savior in this farce of a marriage.

"Doctor Carmichael, we will start with your examination," Mrs. Pratt said, and my gaze darted to hers.

I froze in place. Examination? Here? With these men? Curling up my shoulders, I tried to shield myself as much as possible. The doctor took a step toward me and I jumped back.

"Wait," Mr. Kane interrupted, holding up his hand, halting the other man's steps. I recognized his voice from the auction. "Don't you want to see the man you're marrying?" The man's voice was deep and stern and I realized he was speaking to me. A British accent laced his words, the vowels short and clipped. What was an Englishman doing so far from home, and in a brothel and wedding a complete stranger? The way he'd ignored not only Mrs. Pratt but the doctor as well, was indicative of his power, which had me curious about the man and fearful at the same time.

I shut my eyes briefly and swallowed. I couldn't avoid him any longer. Turning, I looked forward, but only looked upon the buttons of his white shirt. Tilting my chin up, I took the first glimpse of my groom, and sucked in a breath. The first thing I observed was his eyes. Dark, so dark as to be black, with a strong brow. He looked upon me with such intensity, such possession, that it was hard to even glance away. His hair was equally dark, so black as almost to have a blue cast. It was close cut on the sides, longer on top to fall over his forehead. His nose was narrow, but had a slight crook in it, as if being broken at some point. His jaw was wide, angular with a hint of dark whiskers. His lips were full and the corner tipped up as if he knew I was impressed by what I saw.

He was handsome, so very handsome. And tall – well over six feet – and also quite large. His shoulders were wide and defined beneath his white shirt, his chest broad, tapering to a narrow waist. His legs were long and blatantly muscular, something I hadn't noticed in the other room. If he hadn't spoken, I would not have known he was a foreigner.

In comparison to his large size, I was small, dainty even. This man, *my groom,* could hurt me easily if that was his desire, however the smoldering look in his eyes told me he wanted to fulfill other desires. With me. I gulped.

"There now. I can see your face. For such dark hair, your eyes are a surprising blue."

His cultured voice, although rough and a deep baritone, had an undercurrent of something – tenderness, perhaps – which was unexpected. His lip turned up at the corner and a dimple formed in his cheek.

"What is your name?" he queried.

"Emma. Emma James," I replied, his soft tone compelling it from me.

"I am Whitmore Kane, but everyone calls me Kane."

Kane. My groom's name was Kane and he was English. Would he take me off to England to live? The idea struck fear in me. I knew nothing about England, nothing about life outside of the Montana Territory.

"Ian," he said. The man in the corner stepped forward, pulled a folded stack of bills from his pants pocket, counted out an outlandish sum, then handed it to Mrs. Pratt. Was this man Kane's secretary just like Allen was for Thomas?

"We will not require the doctor's services," the man called Ian said to Mrs. Pratt once the transaction was complete. He was tall and broad as well, with light hair and serious eyes.

"You do not wish for me examine her to verify her virginity?" the doctor asked, as if I weren't even in the room. "It is a simple task. She will lie upon the chaise holding her knees up to her chest. I will put my fingers within to feel for the barrier. Surely you'll want proof after the tidy sum you've paid."

I blanched at the very idea the doctor presented. He wanted to touch me with three other men looking on, plus Mrs. Pratt? I took a step back and bumped into Ian. Thankfully, he was the one who'd said that unpleasant task was not necessary. Even so, I gasped at the contact and moved away. The room was too small!

"I assure you I can examine her myself," Kane countered.

The doctor did not look bothered by the response, only nodded his head in understanding. "Certainly."

"Let me get the door for ye, Doctor, so ye can be on yer way," Ian said congenially, his brogue thick.

Dr. Carmichael took a black satchel from Mrs. Pratt's desk and exited the door that Ian held open for him, then closed it firmly behind him.

I exhaled a pent up breath. Just having that man from the room eased some of my tension.

Mrs. Pratt turned to the Justice Of The Peace. "It appears we are ready for you, Mr. Molesly."

No, the tension had not diminished after all. I was going to marry a strange Englishman.

"After, I'd be happy to take you downstairs to avail yourself of one of my girls."

"Is Rachelle available?" he asked, his eyes bright with eagerness.

Mrs. Pratt nodded. "Most assuredly. She has been asking after you."

The man puffed up like a peacock at the flattering, yet most likely false, words. It did make the man eager to complete his task, however. It only led me to question to depth of his calling. He cleared his throat and began. "Dearly beloved...."

This morning I was an heiress eating her breakfast. And now, I stood in nothing but my shift and married a handsome stranger who had bought me at auction in the upstairs of a brothel.

CHAPTER THREE

EMMA

"You wish to inspect your purchase now, I'm sure," Mrs. Pratt commented. She'd ushered the Justice Of The Peace downstairs and in the direction of Rachelle. He had no qualms about performing the unusual ceremony, a task he'd most likely done before; no doubt Rachelle's services were always complimentary after.

Ian moved to stand beside Kane. Both were tall, broad shouldered. I had no knowledge of their profession, but it was most certainly something that involved using their muscles as they were both well formed. Brawny, even. These were not typical gentlemen who sat idly. By their bearing, the intensity they exuded, they were powerful men. And one of them was my husband. The other, he looked upon me in the same possessive glint. I also found them both very handsome.

"I do," Kane replied.

My eyes widened and my mouth fell open, and I retreated, a hand out in a poor reflection of defense. "Surely you don't expect–"

Kane held up his own hand to halt my words. "Wedding me undoubtedly prevented you from an unsavory situation in which you found yourself. I paid a hefty sum in doing so. Therefore, I have earned the right to inspect the merchandise."

Merchandise? My cheeks heated this time not from humiliation but indignation. "I am not some prized mare purchased for breeding."

Kane's dark brow arched. He pierced me with his equally dark eyes. "Aren't you?"

His words left me speechless and I turned away, not able to look at him.

"Here." Mrs. Pratt offered a glass jar to Ian. "This will ease the way."

"No need," Kane replied. "Her cunny will be wet when I check her."

Cunny? I'd never heard that term before, yet I knew it to be crude and an English euphemism for my woman's core. I pressed my legs together. He was going to stick his fingers in me. *There.* I had no idea what he was saying about being wet, but the man seemed confident.

"Nay worries, lass. Kane will have ye likin' it, to be sure. Leave us, please, Mrs. Pratt," Ian said. Not Kane, but Ian. He meant to remain within? Now? I swallowed down my fear of this dominant duo.

Us? I highly doubted I would like Kane to touch me as he planned. Handsome or not, I was wary, and rightly so. Today was too great a transition for me to be anything but.

Mrs. Pratt left readily enough; she'd made her money and was rid of me very tidily. With the vows said, not only legal but binding in God's eyes as well, Kane couldn't change his mind.

The three of us remained, the room less crowded, yet with Kane and Ian's large size, I felt overly small. Threatened, overpowered.

"You are displeased in your husband?" Kane asked, humor lacing his voice.

The tone had me spinning around to face him, but saw from his expression that was what he'd intended. He wanted me to look at him. At both of them.

"With what you intend to do, yes."

"We are your husbands. We *will* touch you."

My eyes widened and I stepped away, now truly fearful. "*We*? Both of you? I must have misheard."

Both men shook their heads. "You did not." Kane pointed to himself, then at Ian. "*We* are your husbands."

That was preposterous and I was sure the expression on my face showed that. "I can't have *two* husbands!"

"Ye are legally wed to Kane, lass, yet ye are mine as well. I am Ian Stewart." Ian's voice was deeper than Kane's, darker and had a stronger accent.

I shook my head, the tears I'd held at bay for so long now filled my eyes, spilled over to run down my cheeks. "Why? I don't understand."

"As you can tell by our accents, we are British."

"Speak for yerself," Ian muttered. "I'm a Scot."

"I...I don't want to live in England," I said, shaking my head vehemently as I did so.

"Neither do we. We might be from another country, but we are home here in the Montana Territory."

He didn't seem the type of man to deceive, so I felt a small kernel of hope that I would not be living in a foreign country. I was only *married* to foreigners. What an insane notion!

Kane crossed his arms over his broad chest. "We're army men. Our lives have been spent defending the realm for Queen and country. This included a stretch in the small middle eastern country of Mohamir which broadened our perspective on the treatment and ownership of women."

Mohamir? I'd never heard of it, however I was not familiar with the further reaches of geography. "Ownership?"

Ian casually tossed the jar from hand to hand as he would a snowball in winter. "A wife belongs to her husband, ye ken? He can do with her as he sees fit. Abuse her, beat her, treat her poorly. Nothing can stop him, neither law nor God can protect a woman from her husband."

I felt all color drain from my face and I stumbled back. These men were like Thomas. Mrs. Pratt promised I would not suffer the fate Ian detailed. He stepped forward and took my elbow, his grip surprisingly gentle considering his size, his grim words.

"Easy, lass," he murmured.

"Please...please don't hurt me," I whispered, my face turned away, flinching from whatever the man would do to me next. I couldn't survive two men abusing me.

Kane stepped closer and I lifted my hand to cover my face.

"Emma. Emma, lass, look at me." Ian's voice was insistent, yet his hold remained gentle. Turning my head ever so slightly, I glanced at him – them – through my lashes. Both observed me intently, their jaws clamped tightly, a cord in Ian's neck bulging.

"We will never beat ye. Never be cruel," Ian vowed. "We will value and respect ye in the ways of the East. Ye will be cherished and protected."

"By both of us," Kane added, his words solemn. "As our wife, you belong to us. It is our job to keep you safe, to see to your happiness, to your pleasure. Beginning now."

"By validating my virginity. You doubt me and Mrs. Pratt," I countered.

"You will find pleasure when I find that validation, I guarantee." Kane sighed, probably when he saw the skepticism on my face. "Mrs. Pratt would not have left the room if she acted falsely, but I will know the truth. We will not leave this place until I do so."

"Why?" I asked, confused. Why did he need confirmation? "We are married and there's no undoing the vows. I am your wife, virgin or not." I glanced at both men as I said the last.

"We must know if you are a virgin so when we take you the first time, we do it right."

Not knowing what he meant, I asked, "You won't take my word on the matter?"

"We don't know you," Kane countered. "And we will change that readily enough."

I retreated a step, looked up at the man to whom I now belonged, eyes wide with fear. "You...you would force me?"

Ian and Kane glanced at each other, speaking without words, it seemed. Ian looked at the glass jar in his hand, considered something, then placed it on the desk.

"I will say this again," Kane repeated. "I am your husband. Ian is your husband. You will do as we bid in all things, but I can assure you, as can Ian, there will be no need for force. You will be well satisfied before we are done."

So arrogant! "Oh? And why is that?"

"Because you will be wet and want our hands on you. I am going to sink my fingers into your cunny to find your maidenhead and you will want them there. Then I will give you your first pleasure. Are you wet now?"

"You keep talking about being wet." I furrowed my brow in confusion. "I...I don't know what you mean."

Instead of approaching me, he moved to the comfortable chair in the corner and sat down. He leaned back, his forearms resting casually on the padded arms, his legs wide and stretched out before him.

"Mrs. Pratt said you watched a couple fucking and this is why you are here." My eyes widened, but he continued. "Were they in bed?"

"No! You are insinuating I snuck in and hid."

"They let you watch then?" Ian asked, still standing beside me.

"No!" I repeated, becoming fretful at the two men hounding me with their words. "I returned to the house and found them...in the kitchen."

"Ah. Did you see his cock?"

I didn't know how to answer this. Of course I saw his cock. They'd been...fucking! Would it make me soiled goods if I said yes?

"Was he fucking her cunny? Her mouth? Her arse?" Kane wondered.

"Mr. Kane, please!" I cried, my cheeks heating. I covered

them with my palms. How could they talk about this so readily?

"Was her cunny wet, lass?" Ian prodded.

"I don't know–"

"Betwixt her legs." He cut me off, his voice deep. "Was she wet betwixt her legs?"

"Yes," I replied, frustrated and unused to being verbally bullied.

"Right now, is your cunny wet like hers was?"

I took another step back and I bumped into the desk. Grabbing hold, I clenched the wooden edge behind me. It was steadying – something to hold onto while my world spun around me. The question was, would it ever right itself?

"Of course not."

"Then I will get you wet so my fingers can slide in easily," Kane replied confidently.

"Why is it so important, this...being wet?" I asked, waving my hand before me.

"It tells us you are aroused. It is a sign, an indication of what arouses you, even when you may tell us otherwise."

"What? No." When he didn't move, didn't say anything, I continued. "I didn't want this. I didn't ask to be here. Thomas drugged me and I woke up here, the only option was to work for Mrs. Pratt or to marry you. I didn't want to do either, nor marry either of you. *Both* of you. How can you expect me to be aroused when it was not my choice?"

"Who is Thomas?" Ian asked, his eyes narrowed.

"My step-brother."

"He's the one you saw fucking?" Kane asked.

I licked my lips. "I saw his secretary first with one of the maids, then when he was done, Thomas took his turn, but I was caught and fled before I witnessed much of that."

Ian nodded. "I ken now. Your step-brother dinna sound like an honorable man. There's nay wonder ye are wary of men."

"You may not want it – this marriage or anything we do to you – your mind may be telling you to resist out of how you perceive you should react, but your body will show us the truth," Kane said.

I was skeptical. Doubtful. Was this what he spoke of? How my mind was questioning him, but could my body go against my very wishes and act at his command? It was impossible, yet so was being married to two men. I could control myself. I crossed my arms firmly over my chest. "How?"

"I know you're afraid." He paused, watched me closely. When I took a deep breath and nodded, he continued. "Answer my questions. I won't even touch you as I do so." He leaned forward, hands on knees and looked up at me, his dark gaze engaging.

"You won't touch me?" I repeated, wanting him to confirm what he said. It raised my hopes, but I let my pessimism show on my face, especially when I looked to Ian.

"Neither of us will. Yet," he clarified. "When your body is ready, then I will find your maidenhead."

I continued to eye him skeptically, doubting him as my body would never be ready, but he was so confident in this!

"Tell me, Emma, what did ye like about watching the couple fuck?" Ian asked. He moved to lean against the wall, ankles crossed, his stance relaxed. Positioned as he was by the door, there was no escape. "Nay your step-brother. The other."

I glanced at a letter opener on the table, my bare feet, the unlit fireplace, everywhere but at him. Them. My sensibilities were being tested.

"Answer me, please."

I couldn't avoid a response. It appeared he had a well of patience and would get what he wanted. They both did. As they said, I belonged to them. Oh dear lord, *them*! Kane's tone – the way he positioned himself across the room, the way Ian stood so casually – made them unthreatening, as if this was their intention. Even so, it was impossible to forget their purpose. This gentle approach was a plan to win me over, and it was only a matter of time before their real ways would come to light. This couldn't be as simple as just two men wanting me.

"I was returning for a child's lunch pail and at first didn't know what I was witnessing." When they quietly watched me with penetrating, dark gazes but did not respond, I continued. "It caught me by surprise. I never expected, never *knew,* this could occur in the kitchen."

"You didn't answer my question, but I'll let it pass. How was he fucking her?" Kane asked.

I closed my eyes briefly, completely unaccustomed to this line of query. "She was...on her back on the table. He held her ankles up and spread wide. His member–"

"Cock." I jumped when Ian said the word, interrupting me. "His cock. Say it, lass."

I licked my lips. "His...cock was big and hard and red and he was putting it in her, over and over."

"He was fucking her cunny with his cock." He said the words I couldn't.

I pushed a curl back from my face. "Yes."

"The woman was enjoying his attentions?"

I looked to Kane at his question, met his stare. "Yes. Yes, she was."

"Did you enjoy watching?"

I pushed off the edge of the desk, paced the small room, from the unlit fireplace to the bookshelf and back, steering clear of Ian. I couldn't tell them the truth. What would they think of me? I would be just like the girls below stairs if I admitted I'd felt...need course through me at their actions.

"Emma?"

"No. No, I didn't," I replied, averting my gaze.

"Emma." This time, when he said my name, it was laced with harshness, disappointment. "I will offer you this one opportunity to lie to me. In the future, if you lie, I promise you will not enjoy the consequences."

"How do you know I'm lying?" I waved my arms in the air. "Isn't it possible that I didn't like what I'd witnessed?"

"As I said before, your body doesn't lie. Look at your nipples, they're hard."

I glanced down. They were.

"Your eyes, they're not a pale blue now, but a deep, stormy gray. I'd say just thinking about what the secretary did to the woman has you aroused. Answer the question, Emma."

I spun around, faced Kane, narrowing my eyes. I didn't need to glance down at my breasts to know the tips were hard. I could feel them, painfully erect. I was not one to let my ire show – no lady of good breeding did – but I'd had quite the day and they'd pushed me too far. "Yes! I enjoyed it. I felt...something when I watched them." I tightened my hands into fists. "Now you know the truth, but it's too late." My breasts were rising and falling beneath my thin shift and the material chafed my sensitive nipples.

Kane only arched a brow at my heated response. Why did he have to be so calm? "Too late?"

"You're married to a woman who is just as her step-brother painted: a voyeur with the moral leanings of a prostitute. Why you would want me, both of you, is beyond me. There's no escaping marriage to me now." No doubt he could hear the bitterness in my tone.

My words did not have the effect I expected. Instead of anger, they were both amused. Kane smiled, broadly, showing off his straight, white teeth. He was even more handsome, and that irked me.

"That's true. You are mine." He still rested his forearms on his knees. "You are Ian's as well." He let those words settle for a moment, perhaps trying to ease my worries. It was not working.

"I will make this even easier for you. Answer yes or no to my questions, all right?"

I took a deep breath and stood before him, yet still too far away for him to reach. Either man could move quickly and grab me, hit me, hurt me, but they remained still. My heart pounded, my breathing deep from my outburst.

"Close your eyes. Go on, close them," Kane added when I didn't respond immediately.

The darkness was like a protective barrier, something I could hide behind. I didn't have to look at Kane or Ian, see their handsome faces, feel their scrutiny with my eyes closed. It was...easier.

"Good girl. Picture the couple. The secretary and the maid. Did your body warm watching them?" His voice slowed, went smoother.

"Yes."

"Did your nipples tighten?"

"Yes."

"Did you want the man to fuck you?" Ian asked, his voice coming from my side.

I pictured Allen and what I saw. *He* hadn't appealed to me, what he'd been doing had. I hadn't wanted him to fuck me, but a man of my own. "No."

"But you wanted to be fucked, to know what it felt like when his cock was buried deep. What the woman felt?"

I saw Clara's head tossed back, eyes closed, mouth open, back arched off the table. She'd been lost in her pleasure in that moment. "Yes."

I heard Kane stand, walk behind me. Circle me.

"Keep your eyes closed." His voice came from the right. "Your cunny – your pussy, that place between your thighs, does it ache at the idea of cock?"

It did. Oh, it did. "Yes."

I heard Ian move next, coming from my left to stand behind

me. "I can see your nipples, all tight and erect." He was close enough to where I could feel his breath on my shoulder. "Do they need to be touched?"

My head fell back, as I became entranced by his deep voice. "Yes."

"Answer my question again, Emma. Are you wet?" Kane asked.

Now, I knew to what he spoke. That place at the juncture of my legs, my woman's place, was...wet. I could feel the hotness of it, the way my folds were swollen and coated in a slick essence brought about by the men's words, the mental pictures they'd elicited, their voices, their very presence.

I was surrounded. I felt the heat from their bodies, the way they took away all the air from the room. With my eyes closed, I didn't feel threatened – overwhelmed, assuredly – but protected instead.

It was dark with my lids closed, only a soft flickering of orange light seeped through. I could block out the world, everything that had happened to me, everything around me except Kane and Ian. Their words, their deep, almost hypnotic voices with the lovely accents. This was why I felt at liberty to answer, to respond to how they made me feel.

I heard Kane sink back into the chair in front of me. Waiting.

"Yes," I uttered.

"Open your eyes," Kane commanded.

My lashes fluttered open as I looked down at him first, then glanced over my shoulder at Ian whose gaze was dark and lust filled. He was close, only a foot away, but he did not touch me. Neither had yet to touch me except for when Ian caught my stumble.

"Come here," Kane ordered. He gestured with his hand to the space before him, his knees wide, the fabric of his pants stretched taut and defined over his muscular thighs.

I approached him slowly and stood where he bid. He met my eyes, then his head lowered, taking in my breasts and tight nipples, the transparent shift, my bare thighs.

"Spread your legs."

I moved my left leg so my stance was wider, my thigh bumping against his knee, and waited. What did he intend? He still hadn't touched me in any way. My modesty was losing to curiosity. Neither had done anything for me to fear, so on bated breath, I waited.

Slowly, he lifted his right hand and slipped it between my legs, up beneath the short hem of my shift to touch me. *There.*

I startled at the contact. The one finger brushed over me in the lightest of touches, yet it felt like I was being branded, the heat that it wrought searing. I gasped and met his piercing, dark gaze, but didn't move, afraid that if I did he might stop. With a feather light touch, he slid over my folds, slowly, watching me.

The corner of his mouth tipped up in something akin to triumph all the while learning my flesh.

"I haven't held your hand. I haven't kissed you. I like knowing that the first place I touch your body is your delectable cunny."

When his finger flicked over the place that throbbed, that had pulsed and come to life when I'd witnessed Clara and Allen, a moan slipped from my lips. Panic flared in my eyes at the illicit feelings, the way I found pleasure in a stranger's intimate touch. That barest of caresses felt so incredibly...amazing, that I feared it. Feared what he was doing to me. How could a man I didn't know bring about such carnal feelings with the barest of touches? It wasn't proper. It was wrong.

I started to step back, but just one word from his lips kept me still.

"No." Somehow, after only a few minutes, he was able to sense my emotions. "I will give you your pleasure. Do not fear it, or me." His jaw was tight, his gaze hooded as his fingers became bolder, parting my folds and running over the slippery, swollen flesh. Finding my virgin opening, he circled it, nudging in just a fraction and my body clenched down on it.

"She's so tight, Ian," he murmured.

I'd forgotten about the other man.

The finger dipped in even further, then slid back out to slide up my folds to the bundle of nerves. I exhaled harshly and placed my hands on Kane's solid shoulders for balance. My knees weakened and I needed to hold on to stay upright. Just the very tip of his finger on me had me off kilter. Even through the jacket of his suit, I could feel his warmth, the very strength of him.

When his finger moved back to my opening, another finger joined and two slipped inside. I shifted my hips and lifted up onto my toes at the onslaught. My tissues burned at the stretching and yet, it felt...exquisite. I could hear how wet I was, the sound of his fingers probing me filled the space between us.

"There." His eyes held mine. I couldn't look away. I felt the pressure and pain of his digits as they tried to push even further into me, but couldn't. I clenched his shoulders and winced. "I can feel her maidenhead."

"I...." I licked my lips. "I told you I was a virgin."

"Yes, yes you did. Now I have to decide what to do about it." He pulled his fingers completely from me and I was bereft, lost. Empty.

His fingers were glistening and slick with my wetness and I watched as Kane put them in his mouth and licked them. "So sweet. Like honey." His gaze heated, his skin flushing in what I recognized as desire. "Taste."

My eyes widened. "Your fingers?"

He shook his head. "No. Kiss me."

I leaned forward ever so slightly and Kane came the rest of the way so his mouth covered mine. It wasn't a tentative, chaste kiss, for his mouth opened over mine and his tongue delved deep. He tasted musky and sweet and deliciously male, perhaps a combination of my woman's essence and his own personal flavor. I sank into the kiss, I could do nothing but, for he was quite skilled at it. My body heated and softened, my skin warming and becoming sensitive to the cool air. Finally, after an interminable length of time, Kane sat back.

"Run your fingers over your pussy. Good girl. Now feed them to Ian. Let him taste you, too."

I pulled my hand from between my trembling thighs and looked at my coated fingers. My arousal was warm and slick. Ian took my hand in his and lifted it to his mouth, sucking on my wet digits. His pale eyes darkened as I felt him suck on the tips of my fingers. My mouth fell open as I watched him.

"Aye, like honey," he said when he lowered my hand back to my side. His voice was darker, more gravelly than before, his accent stronger. "Have you ever come before?"

I didn't know to what he spoke, but I had no doubt the answer was no, so I shook my head as I licked my lips.

"Then for being such a good girl, you will have a treat," Kane promised.

Both of his hands moved beneath my shift and over my cunny, or the other word he'd used, my pussy. Fingers dipped inside of me, just bumping into my maidenhead, while his other hand moved to circle and flick at the bundle of nerves that had my eyes slipping closed, my head falling back and mouth opening to let a moan of pleasure escape.

This was what Clara had been feeling: sheer, unadulterated bliss. Kane was masterfully working my body as a weapon against my strongest of mental defenses. One flick of a well skilled finger and my mind emptied of every reason why this was wrong.

This was something I couldn't control. In this moment, my body did not belong to me. It belonged to Kane.

I shook my head at that revelation. "No, please. I'm scared," I cried out, my hands pushing on his shoulders one moment, then gripping and clinging to him the next.

"There's nothing to fear, lass," Ian murmured from behind me.

"I've got you," Kane added. "You are safe and in this moment, your body belongs to me."

It was too much. The pleasure was building, growing. Kane was masterful in working my body. My skin was damp, my knees were weak, my nipples tight peaks. I felt engulfed in flames and with each stroke of Kane's fingers he threw more fuel on the fire, until....

"Come, Emma," Ian ordered. "Let us see your pleasure."

His commanding voice pushed me over some precipice and I was falling, falling into nothingness. The intensity of it all was so grand that I screamed and clawed at Kane's shoulders. With letting go, giving over to what he was doing to me, I'd found the most amazing pleasure I never knew was possible.

No wonder Clara had spread her legs. No wonder she let herself be taken on the kitchen table. With this one demonstration of Kane's power, I was addicted. I wanted more. I wanted it again. I *needed* what he'd just done to me. Again and again.

Kane's fingers continued to gently stroke and work my body until I'd taken a deep breath and opened my eyes. Kane watched me and the corner of his mouth turned up, dimple appearing. "Like that, did you?"

I almost purred like a cat and couldn't help but grin. "Oh, yes."

Pulling his hands free, he showed me the evidence of my desire, what I tasted even now on my tongue from our kiss. "You dripped all over my hands. You will always be wet for me."

CHAPTER FOUR

KANE

The simple shift so seductively wrapping Emma's body was more alluring than any lacy garb worn by Mrs. Pratt's girls. If I hadn't just found the proof of her innocence, I would think her a temptress. Her coral nipples poked at the thin fabric, the soft swells of her breasts were plump above the plain edge. Her skin was pale and creamy, most assuredly silky to the touch.

"I want to see all of ye, lass. Let's take off your shift," Ian told her.

Her skin was damp and flushed with desire, her eyes cloudy with her first pleasure. There was no doubt that had been her first orgasm, for she'd been so quick to arouse, so fearful of the pleasure. And yet, when she came, she succumbed to it beautifully. Emma looked at me now with those bewitching blue eyes for a moment, a small frown marring her smooth skin.

"Show us what's ours, Emma."

But I hadn't touched. I hadn't touched her anywhere but her cunny and kissed her delectable mouth. Her skittishness endeared her to me and I felt a swift and ruthless wave of possessiveness at the very first glimpse. When I tasted her essence from her fingers, my cock pulsed against my pants because her scent, the taste of her cunny had me wanting to sink into her sweet depths. I knew Ian felt the same way, although neither of us had said as much.

Mrs. Pratt's auction was known to only a small group of men who traveled in similar circles as Ian and I. Landowners, ranchers, mine owners, railroad magnates whose actions were often outside the parameters of the law – men able to keep silent about their lives, about how they, or their fellow businessmen, acquired their wives. Ian and I had secrets – that's why we settled as far from England as possible and in such a remote a location.

All bidders were wealthy men who sought more than a quick fuck. Malcolm Pierce was looking for a bride to be his little girl, to dress her up and treat her as a child, yet fuck like a woman. Alfred Potter's mansion in Billings was filled with female servants who tended to more than just the house. Since he needed an heir, a bride was required, but she would be only one of several women who serviced him in his household. John Rivers liked doling out pain more than pleasure and his bride would need a strong constitution and a wild spirit.

We'd heard about the auction while playing cards downstairs as several of Mrs. Pratt's girls shared their attentions with Ian and me. It was Mrs. Pratt's invitation to claim a virgin bride that had piqued our interest, especially when we learned of the other bidders. An auction of this type was common in the Mohamir where we'd been stationed for several years – an auction for a woman trained from birth to please several husbands, to submit to them for their protection as well as their pleasure. Those women knew the men who would win them would treat them with honor. This auction could offer no such guarantee.

Our years abroad in the army reinforced the idea this antiquated approach was, for Ian and me, as well as a handful of other members of our regiment, the best option. Life as a soldier was short; having more than one husband offered protection and stability to the woman and their children. These unusual ways swayed us from following the strict Victorian dictates and morals of our country. But it was the actions of our superiors that had us leaving the ranks, abandoning our positions in the British army and escaping to the United States.

When I first laid eyes on Emma, I knew she was for us. The other men could find their own woman another time.

When she was too slow to comply to my command to remove her shift, Ian stepped forward, his fingers dipping to the hem of the barrier that prevented us from seeing her body. As his fingers slid the material up her thighs, she jerked in surprise, but held still.

Slowly, Ian lifted the material up to show off her shapely legs, the dark hair at the apex of her thighs that glistened with her desire, her narrow waist, flat belly, full breasts with large, tight nipples. The soft cotton caught on her hair and a long curl fell free as Ian tossed the shift onto the floor.

Seeing her naked, I knew we'd made the right choice. This was our first auction, and most definitely our last. Where Mrs. Pratt found her women to be sold off was not asked, but it was clear to both Ian and me that Emma was as innocent as could be. Seeing her dark hair, her creamy skin, the slightly hidden delights of her body, she was perfection. Seeing the fear and shame on her face had every protective and possessive instinct screaming to save her. The reason was clear, at least to me. She wasn't meant for the other men at the auction. This woman was ours. And so I bid, and bid well.

When the doctor had prepared to inspect Emma, to put his fingers in her cunny, I saw red. Ian would not have allowed another man to touch her either, especially now when every soft inch of her was visible. I knew Carmichael well. He was a skilled doctor who tended to patients all over the area, but he also enjoyed new flesh. That bent was fine for other women, but Emma's cunny was for Ian and me alone. I wanted our hands upon her to be the first. Her last. What we planned for her wasn't always gentle, wasn't tame or legal by society's standards, but we'd kill any man who touched our bride. A Mohamiran woman was never abused, never mistreated, only treasured. We would give Emma the same honor. She was scared of us now, but once she learned of our intentions, was trained to our ways, she'd see our devotion.

She stood naked within the circle of my legs. Her skin was unmarred and porcelain white and I itched to feel its silkiness.

Her breasts were a handful, teardrop shaped with nipples I longed to suck and nip. But none of that was the prize. It was at the juncture of her thighs, hidden well in the dark curls. I could just make out the pink cunny lips, all swollen and slick from my touch. Her clit protruded, a hard pink nub that was the epicenter of her desire.

Emma would be responsive; I had no doubt. She might have been skittish as we'd visually inspected her, then bid on her, but her passion couldn't be hidden. And once I'd won the bidding and she'd looked at me, I was certain. The way her eyes sparked with indignation, frustration and then ultimately desire – I hadn't been mistaken. Ian saw it, too. I recognized the need for her in his eyes, the tense jaw, the fisted hands, for all of his actions mirrored mine. I was the one who had legally wed her, but Ian would claim her in the most elemental of ways and Emma would never doubt his possession of her.

She would make the perfect wife, responsive and eager to please without even realizing. She just needed some guidance from her men. Since I showed her first pleasure, let her see how I controlled her body, it was time for her to tend to me. My cock was hard enough to pound nails in a fence post and my wife's first lesson would be how to slake my need. Ian would have his turn next.

"Have you ever touched a cock before?" Ian asked, his voice husky.

I undid my belt, the placket of my pants. Emma tilted her

head and watched as I pulled my cock free. I couldn't help the sigh that escaped as it bobbed free from the tight confines of my pants.

"No," she whispered, eyes wide. "You...you're...you're so big." She darted a glance over her shoulder at Ian. He was still clothed, but the thick outline of his cock was evident beneath his pants and I knew by Emma's deep inhale that she hadn't missed it.

I smiled wickedly and met her gaze when she turned her head back. "The vows have been said, Emma. There's no need for flattery."

"That's supposed to...to go in me?" She looked at me with equal measures of surprise and concern.

"Will. It *will* go in you. Right now, in fact." Wrapping one hand around her waist, I pulled her forward as I leaned back, settled into the chair. She gasped as she lost her balance. "Sit astride me."

Placing her hand once again on my shoulder, she placed one knee on the outside of my thigh, then the other, her breasts directly in front of my face. I couldn't deny such a tempting offer and pulled one pink tip into my mouth. The tip was soft at first, but hardened quickly against my tongue. Her skin was warm, her taste sweet, her response a delight.

"Oh!" she cried as my hand on her waist held her in place, sucking and drawing on the hard tip. Her hands moved to my shoulders, her fingers digging into the tense muscles there.

Her skin smelled of flowers and arousal, a heady combination. At one extra strong suck, Emma's fingers slid upward to tangle in my hair, holding my head in place. Her breath escaped in little pants as I trailed kisses from one breast to the other, ensuring that each nipple received the same attentions. Her hips began to shift of their own volition and her knees squeezed against my sides.

"She's ready," Ian said gruffly. He looked at me from over Emma's shoulder just before he lowered his mouth to kiss and nibble at her neck.

I pulled away and saw that her nipples were wet and bright pink from my mouth. "Emma, look at me. Look at me when I make you mine."

My hand slid from her waist and down to the soft globe of her arse as I lined my cock up. My blunt head slipped through her drenched folds and settled at her virgin opening and I gritted my teeth at the scalding hot feel of her. Ian didn't stop running his hands over her body, his mouth on her heated skin.

Emma's eyes opened at the placement and looked at me, uncertainty flaring. "Kane, I don't think--"

"Don't think, love. Feel. Feel Ian's mouth on your skin, feel his hands run over your body, cup your breasts."

Her eyes slipped closed as she did just that. "You're too big. You won't fit. And Ian's watching!"

I pushed her down onto my cock as I thrust my hips up, filling her only with the head, her maidenhead blocking further penetration. Her eyes widened at the feel of being stretched wide.

"I'll fit, and Ian will claim you next."

Ian's hands came around to cup her breasts, to pinch her nipples.

She shook her head and frantically pushed up with her knees, fighting me. "No! It's too much."

Her squirming wasn't going to have me pull out. In fact, quite the opposite. Her writhing had her inner walls clenching and squeezing down on the tip of my cock, driving me insane.

"Stop," Ian commanded. Realizing she was panicking, he spanked her arse, her skin quivering beneath his palm.

She froze in place and cried out. Stunned. "He spanked me!"

"He bloody well did, and he will do it again if you continue to resist. Oh, you liked it. Ian, she's dripping onto my lap."

"No, I don't like it!" she cried out, but her juices dripping onto my cock said otherwise.

Ian gave her another mild spank. "Do not lie, lass."

Her inner walls clenched down on the head of my cock. I gritted my teeth. "You are not in control here. We are. I assure you my cock will fit and your body is most assuredly wet and ready. It is your maidenhead that is blocking the way. I will solve that problem right now."

"But–"

Before she could protest anymore, I pressed her down with both hands on her arse, thrusting up, deliberately hard, claiming her. She was more fearful of the idea than the act itself, therefore I resolved the problem at hand. I breached her maidenhead with that one thrust and my cock pushed through from just the entrance all the way in to the hilt. She cried out and stiffened, her face contorting in pain,her eyes as wide as saucers at being stuffed so completely. She held still, but her fingers dug little furrows into my shoulders.

The feel of being embedded within her hot cunny was so incredible that I groaned. Her walls milked my cock, the wetness almost scalding. I could feel the entrance to her womb nudging against my wide head. I was so deep and she was so tight.

"I fit," I hissed.

Swallowing visibly, she replied, "Yes. Yes, you do. Is that it? Are you done?" She was panting, as if afraid to breathe too deeply.

"Done?" Ian asked, his hands soothing her as if she were a skittish mare. "You're just getting started, lass."

I grinned at her naïveté. "Now you ride me."

"Ride you? But it hurt." She pouted, clearly afraid to move.

With my palms, I guided her, showing her how. With each slick slide of my cock against her cunny walls, I was close to coming. There was nothing to prevent my balls from tightening, my cock thickening and swelling within her. This would be a fast fuck; she'd tempted me too much.

"Oh," she gasped, the sound escaping was of pleasure, no longer pain.

"Only pleasure now, Emma," Ian promised.

"She's so tight," I murmured, my teeth clenching.

She was a quick learner, shifting her hips and lifting up and down on her knees to ride my cock. I was her stallion and she was the timid mare. As she found her rhythm, I moved my hands to her breasts, cupping them, feeling their weight as I plucked and tugged on the hard tipped nipples. Ian knelt down behind her and reached around between her spread thighs to touch her clit.

"Kane, I...oh my," she sighed, her head falling back. Her hair was a wild tangle down her back.

"See, lass, no more pain. Only pleasure," Ian reiterated as he worked her hard little nub.

"Come again, baby. Come on my cock."

She was a natural at taking orders when her mind was distracted, for she came on command, her cunny walls milking me, strangling my cock in its pulsating grip. I came too, my hips driving up into her hard as my cock spurted thick ropes from my body, filling her with my seed.

The fit was so tight that as she shifted, my cum dripped out, coating her thighs along with her virgin's blood. She slumped down upon me, a warm weight upon my chest. She was a lusty one, easily to orgasm and most certainly claimed. I glanced up at Ian, his need to fuck Emma evident in every line of his body. He nodded his head in silent agreement. She was ours, and his turn was next.

IAN

The sun was shining when Emma finally stirred. She was on her side, her back curled up against my front. She made a sound in her throat and stretched before stiffening, remembering that she was not alone. I'd enjoyed the past few minutes just staring at her, amazed she was mine – mine and Kane's.

After Kane claimed her the night before, we bundled Emma into a long dressing gown supplied by Mrs. Pratt and slipped into the back entrance of the hotel. Neither Kane nor I had had any intention of spending the night in the brothel, no matter how easy it would have been to find an empty room and fuck our bride all night long. Instead, I'd carried her to my hotel room, sight unseen. We hadn't anticipated a bride when we'd taken the trip into town and Kane's room was down the hall. Since he'd claimed her first, she'd been mine for the night. Sharing wasn't an option at the hotel. We ken our marital ways to be honorable, but the people of Simms would not agree. Once on the ranch, however, the two husbands to one bride dynamic would not be hidden.

I'd stripped Emma, who was too tired to put up much of a fight, and helped her beneath the covers before she fell directly asleep. We didna ken her life story prior to the auction other than that of a bastard step-brother, but whatever her day had been like, it had exhausted her. Or perhaps it had been her initiation into fucking that had tired her so. I spent a long night with my cock hard and throbbing, waiting to claim her for myself.

"Good morning, wife," I murmured in her ear. I saw goose flesh rise on her arm above the sheet as my breath fanned over her nape. I smiled into her soft, heated skin.

Once we'd heard of the auction, our sole goal had been to recognize whether the woman up for bid was in danger of the other men, or if it was all an act. One look at her and we'd both known. She'd needed our help. She couldna have not fall into the clutches of the others. She would be ours.

It had been very late when Kane finally fucked her and I'd watched as he took her virginity. The look on her face when she'd been breached by Kane's cock would be something I remembered forever – the look of surprise, a hint of pain and the instant knowledge that she'd been claimed. When she came riding him, her head thrown back, her dark hair spilling down her back, breasts thrust forward, she was the most beautiful thing I'd ever seen.

As I watched her sleep during the night, I considered her safety. It reassured me to ken that Kane would be there for her if the bastard Evers tracked me. We'd crossed an ocean and a continent to avoid the man and the crimes he'd pinned on me years ago. The others in the regiment who'd joined us here in the Montana Territory also had sullied reputations and lost rank, but they weren't wanted as I was. I kent, deep down I kent, Evers would find me. He'd find me and drag me back for trial. There was no question it would be soon. Finding a wife and settling into the happiness I knew would follow, was a luxury Evers would find a way to take from me. And so, my time with her was most assuredly short, and I was reassured to ken that Emma would be safe with Kane.

Many women had come before, for Kane and me, but there was no question Emma was different. Not only did she arouse every sexual need to a point where my balls ached with impatience to have her, but every protective, possessive desire as well. She wasn't a woman to fuck and leave. She was a woman to cherish, to protect, to possess, to dominate. I ran my fingers over her dark curls, silky soft. She was so very dainty. Sweet. Sexy as hell. Fucking her wouldn't be enough. We'd spend time training her to meet our every need, and her every pleasure. This is what husbands did for their wife. It was our job, our responsibility.

She began to stir, and twas time to make her mine. Finally! Later, the training would begin. My cock throbbed against the curve of her arse. When she stiffened in my arms, recognizing she was most certainly not alone and definitely naked, I shifted so that she lay beneath me, her soft breasts pillowing against my chest, her nipples hardening at the contact. I nudged one of my legs between hers and I felt the heat of her cunny against my thigh.

"Oh," she gasped in surprise. Her hands came up to push against my chest. She was so lovely when she awoke, her dark hair spread over the pillow, her pale eyes soft and sleepy.

"Expecting Kane?"

She nodded warily, licked her lips. I bit back a groan at the idea of what that little pink tongue could do.

"Dinna fear any jealousy or Kane's ire. Ye are my wife just as ye are his and he expects ye to be well fucked when we board the stage. By me."

Her eyes widened at my words. I wasn't going to soften them because of her innocence. I would speak and act as I planned to proceed. I would be gentle, however she would know my dominance. Shifting my hips, I nudged my cock against her inner thigh. The skin there was so satiny soft it made my cock pulse.

"We must rise for the stage, but first, I will fuck you, make you mine just as much as Kane's." My voice was deep with desire. "Every morning while ye are still abed, Emma, ye will be fucked either by me or Kane, or both of us together. Trust me in saying that ye will be quite eager for this soon enough as are we. For now, let me get ye ready." I nudged her legs wider and reached between to test her readiness. She gasped in surprise and pushed at me, trying to lift me off. She'd ridden Kane when he took her. This was the first time she was beneath a man. I'd need to take it slow, to wake her body to desire just like she awoke from sleep. When I found her clit, her reticence slipped away, just as her hands dropped to her sides.

Propping myself up onto one arm, I leaned down and kissed her, brushing my lips across her softness, then slipped my tongue in to touch hers. I played with her slick cunny, brushed over her clit all the while I kissed her. Slowly. Leisurely. I felt every tense line of her body soften, felt her skin heat beneath my touch. I brushed her hair off her face then kissed my way across her jaw to her ear, licked the dainty swirl.

"Mmm," I whispered, my cock hardening painfully as I found her dripping wet. Her heat practically scorched my fingers. "You're slick with Kane's seed. I love to ken you're cunny's filled like this. It is my turn to add to it. I have been waiting all night to make you mine."

"Why...." She cleared her throat. "Why didn't you do it last night?" she whispered, tilting her head to the side to give me better access to nuzzle at the frantic pulse beating at her neck. Her scent was so sweet. Tempting. Her hands gripped tightly on my biceps. "Ye were asleep, Emma. I want ye wide awake when we fuck." I moved between her thighs, spread her wide with my palms. "When ye call out my name. Kane may have taken yer virginity, but ye are mine, too."

I looked down her body, noticed her tight nipples and had to taste them. I laved a turgid tip then took it fully into my mouth as I slowly, gently even, slipped a finger deep inside her.

"Ian!" she cried and I relished in hearing my name from her lips, especially in such an aroused tone. I shifted from one breast to the other, the rasp of my beard leaving a hint of red skin in its wake. Her skin was so delicate, almost tender, yet I wanted to fuck her hard. My cock ached to sink into her delicious heat. The way her inner walls were clenching down on my finger, I knew she'd be tight and perfect around my cock.

Her hips began to shift, her skin flushed and dewy, the wetness copious on her thighs. She was ready.

Lifting my head, I looked down into her eyes and saw only pleasure there. No fear, no pain, nothing but need. Lowering my head, I kissed her as I aligned my cock up to nudge at her tight entrance and slid into her in one deep stroke. I swallowed the moan that escaped her lips. She was so tight, her body clamping down on me like a vice, rippling around me. Her hands gripped my back, her nails digging in as I began to move. Neither of us could kiss any longer, focused solely on how we were connected, the way it felt. I grabbed her arse, tilted her up so I penetrated her even deeper. Completely.

Her back arched, her head tilting back as I took her. Her breath escaped in little pants, her eyes closed.

"Look at me, lass."

Her blue eyes fluttered open as I continued to thrust into her. Her hands were once again on my chest trying to push me away. Pull me in. She couldn't decide.

"This isn't right," she moaned, a little frown forming on her brow, confusion warring with the pleasure on her face.

"What?" I rasped.

"This. You. Kane." She exhaled each time I filled her.

"You're going to come, baby. I can feel your walls squeezing me. What shame is there in your pleasure when it is your husbands that give it to you?" Sweat beaded my brow as I held off coming until Emma did. She was close, right on the edge, but she was thinking too much.

"I can't want two men. It makes me...it makes me a harlot."

I grinned at her words. She wanted both of us and that pleased me immensely. My orgasm built at the base of my spine and into my balls. My seed all but boiled and was ready to escape. Not being able to wait any longer, I moved my hand between us so I could rub my thumb over her little distended nub. Breaking her of her inhibitions, her doubts of having two husbands, was not something that I could resolve now. But I could pleasure her, let her see how good it was, not only with

Kane, but with me as well. She would ken we were both well satisfied with her, and she in return. So I worked her clit faster as I filled her over and over. A drop of sweat dripped from my brow and onto an upturned breast.

"No, not a harlot. It makes you our wife," I all but growled as she came. I had to cover her mouth with mine once again to stifle her scream. I wanted to keep her pleasure just for me, like a secret gift I would not share with anyone, most especially the other hotel guests along the hall. She might be modest and uncomfortable in her passion, but when she let go of her inhibitions, she was incredible. So responsive, so sensitive. My own orgasm could not be held back any longer and my seed joined Kane's. My base instinct to claim, to mark, to fill was complete.

CHAPTER FIVE

IAN

"How were you able to claim the coach just for us?" Emma asked, her body shifting and swaying with the poorly sprung motions of the stagecoach. She sat across from both of us, her posture erect, her hands clasped primly in her lap. She hadn't been prim an hour ago. The only outward indication that she'd been recently fucked was a slight flush to her cheeks.

"Money," I replied. The leather flaps were open on only a few of the windows to minimize dust and the interior was warm. The three of us were alone, a large purse to the driver ensured we had privacy for the duration of our journey, not that there was much room for other passengers.

Emma wore a blue silk dress, the bodice low cut enough that the swells of her breasts were plump and full above the lace trimmed edge. The sleeves were long, the waist trim. The fabric and color were decadent and impractical for travel, but certainly showcased our wife's eyes and other attributes. Mrs. Pratt had done as requested and delivered something to wear to the hotel, but it was not the least bit serviceable. When Emma had questioned what had happened to her very serviceable dress she'd been wearing upon her arrival at the brothel, Mrs. Pratt only replied that the alternate dress might please Kane and me more. It certainly kept us focused on her assets. The appreciative look from the coach driver hadn't been missed by me or Kane. We were not the only ones that found Emma beautiful.

"Where is it we are headed?" she asked, her gaze turned towards the window.

"Travis Point," Kane told her. "From there, we will ride the rest of the way to Bridgewater, our ranch, by horse. We have a few hours to fill and there are many very pleasant ways to pass the time."

She sat directly across from me, our knees bumping on occasion. "Pleasant ways? You mean what we did last night?" Her gaze shifted to meet Kane's, then mine. "Or what we did earlier?"

The sun shifted and filled the stage, Emma's body swathed in a stripe of bright sunshine. She was so lovely, so endearing when she looked at us with such questioning glances. Knowing we'd saved her from a less appealing fate made her innocence even more precious.

"There is so much more, lass. Undo the buttons on your dress and show us your beautiful breasts," I commanded.

Her plump lower lip fell open as she looked around. "Here? Now?"

"We are quite alone for the moment and I wish to see your beautiful breasts. Kane?"

"Yes. Your breasts are lovely and shouldn't be hidden from us."

"But–"

"Do not question us, baby. It will please us to see you so," Kane countered, the tone of his voice shifted to commanding. If we wished to see her breasts, we would not be deterred.

She must have heard the sharp bite in his voice because her fingers went up to undo the tiny buttons that ran down the length of her bodice. Slowly, the two sides flapped open, revealing her white corset. I had ensured the fit was quite snug when I dressed her, pulling the laces tight, so I knew her nipples were just below the edge. In fact, I could see the upper curve of one pink tip peeking out above the top.

"Lift your breasts out," I told her. She belonged to both of us – in all things – and the quicker she acclimated to having two men to please, the better. Two men to please, two men to obey. The ranch was a rugged place, where dangers abounded. The land was harsh and rugged. *We* were rugged. She would obey us in the bedroom for her pleasure and outside of it to keep her safe.

As she held my gaze, she tugged the front of the corset down to sit at the bottom curve of her breasts. Cupping herself, she adjusted her soft flesh until it was fully exposed. With the tight corset beneath, her creamy globes were lifted high and thrust out, the soft pink tips plump and pointing straight towards us. I kent how they tasted, how they felt against my tongue. My mouth watered to suckle at them again, but I wanted something else from her first.

"On your knees, lass." I gestured with my chin to the floor between my wide stretched legs.

"Ian," she countered, her eyes flitting left and right, but I arched a brow.

"I can spank you for your disobeying Ian, but you will still end up on your knees before him," Kane said.

Her eyes flared in surprise at his words. "Disobey? You mean–"

"Yes, we would spank you," Kane reiterated.

Licking her lips, she slid off the bench seat, knelt on the wooden floor, and placed her small hands on my thighs. She swayed with the motion of the stage, her face upturned to look at me with sweet innocence. In this position, she was a sight to behold.

Lowering my head, I kissed her, but only chastely and briefly. I wanted to deepen the kiss, but she had a lesson in cock sucking and I didn't want to divert from that. I didn't want anything to delay her hot little mouth around my cock. Her skin was flushed, her breasts were out and on delightful display, her eyes innocent as to what was to come. I loved her submissive placement between my legs, her mouth only inches from my from my–

"Take out my cock." My words were deep, my need obvious not only in my voice but in the thick length pressed against my pants.

With small, fumbling fingers, Emma undid the placket on my pants and pulled me out. I was incredibly hard, the tip oozing clear liquid in a steady stream. I'd fucked her only an hour before, yet I was ready for her again. What man could resist a wife on her knees before him?

"First lesson, lass, is sucking cock."

Her eyes flared as she understood my more crude terminology. "How?"

"Lick the tip. See how it's dripping for you? Clean it off."

She did. Her dainty little tongue lapped at it, swirling around the plum shaped head. My breath hissed out through clenched teeth at the hot lick.

"How do I taste?"

I watched her throat work as she swallowed. "Salty."

"Good girl. Now take it all the way into your mouth."

As instructed, she engulfed me in her hot warmth as far as she could go, which was not all that far, only half of me filled her. Her eyes widened and she coughed, pulling back. "You're too big!" she gasped, her eyes watering.

"Ye will ken soon enough, lass. Ye are doing fine. For now, take me as far as ye can go."

She did, licking and sucking with a sweet innocence that had my hips coming off the seat. "Grab hold of the base." I ground my teeth together as her grip tightened around me. "Good," I growled. "Now fuck my cock with your mouth."

Lowering her head, she took me into her mouth as far as she could comfortably go then pulled back, over and over. Her mouth was so wet and so hot that she all but seared my flesh. She was so earnest, so eager to comply with my instruction that my balls tightened, my orgasm close.

"Her mouth is as tight and perfect as her cunny," I told Kane, savoring the tight suction. I wouldn't last long, the need to come so intense.

"She's being a very good girl," Kane praised as he watched Emma take my cock. His big hand ran over her head, stroked her silky hair in reassurance.

I closed my eyes and gave in to the pleasure of her tentative tongue, the hot licks, the sweet sucking until I was almost there. "I'm going to come in your mouth, lass. Ye need to take it all. Our seed belongs in ye. Your cunny, your mouth, your ass. Swallow it all down."

My hips thrust up to join with the ministrations of her mouth and culminated in the most intense release that I groaned, my fingers gripping the hard bench seat, as my seed shot into the back of Emma's throat. Pulse after pulse, I throbbed against her tongue. She was sucking me dry all the while trying to swallow my seed. All she accomplished with her unskilled actions was choking on the copious seed before backing off my cock, the final white ropes of my cum spurting onto her upturned breasts. My release was explosive and did not seem to end. Some thick cream dripped down her chin and one large glob landed on her plump nipple. The erotic sight of her being marked in such a way prevented my cock from softening.

She'd done an impressive, albeit sloppy job. I came quickly and reveled in her first mouth fucking, my body sated. I had to catch my breath, for she had the ability to render my body useless until I could recover.

Even though she did beautifully, there was a lesson here for Emma to learn and I couldna veer from teaching her what we expected of her just because of her eagerness to please. However, I was too replete to do anything, the haze of lust and release overwhelming. My cock rested half erect against my open pants, wet and shiny from Emma's mouth. My shoulders slid across the seat back with the sway of the coach. Fortunately, Kane recognized my state and took over.

He shook his head in disappointment.

She glanced up at him through her lashes as she lifted her hand to wipe her chin.

"Don't," he told her. He leaned forward and ran his finger over the cooling seed and fed it to her. "Lick." Her lips closed over his finger and she sucked it as if it were a cock. "You disobeyed, Emma."

He pushed a second finger in her mouth to join the first, sliding the digits in and out like I did my cock. Slowly, he worked the fingers further and further back until met with her instinctive reaction to choke. Pressing down on her tongue, he held his fingers in place. "You must adjust to taking a cock. All the way."

Her hands wrapped around his wrist as her eyes widened in panic. She was breathing, air going in and out quickly through her nose, but she fought him and the innate reaction for something to be so deep in her mouth.

"Shh. Settle," Kane murmured, his tone calming her. After only a few seconds, he pulled back, slipped his fingers from her mouth.

"You didn't swallow his seed, baby." He glanced down at her exposed breasts and the viscous cream spread in random pulses across her pale flesh. I liked seeing my seed mark her this way, a stain of possession.

Emma lowered her head to see for herself. "I'm sorry, Kane, Ian, but it was too much. It...it surprised me."

She was correct; my seed had been plentiful. Her lush mouth had pulled it all from me.

"It is your job to do our bidding and you did not."

Her brow furrowed. "I had no idea it would be so...copious.

I now know what to expect, therefore I will do better next time."

Kane stroked her hair again and she tilted her head into the caress, clearly savoring, and even craving, the affection. "Of course you will, but you must be punished."

She sat back on her heels, a frown marring her brow. "Punished? Why?"

"Because you did not swallow Ian's seed."

"But–"

He held up his hand and she quieted. Pulling a handkerchief from the pocket of his suit jacket, Kane wiped at her breasts, smearing away all traces of my emissions.

"Over my lap, please."

She shook her head. "Kane, no. I will be good."

"You were a very good girl, sucking his cock, but we do not take disobedience lightly. We will no longer be in a large town but on a ranch where it is wild and untamed. Following rules can save your life, therefore we must know that you will obey us in all things. It is our job to keep you safe, but your job to listen so we may do so. Now, over my knees." He deepened his voice and hardened his gaze.

She glanced at me, perhaps seeking a pardon.

"Your delay has added five additional strikes of Kane's palm," I told her. "Would ye like to delay longer and make it ten?"

She scurried to obey, realizing the consequence was growing. When she positioned herself correctly, her belly pressing into Kane's thighs, her feet just touched the floor of the stage on one side, her hair a curtain about her head on the other. I could see her breasts pointing downwards, the nipples tight and furled. I had to shift my legs out of the way to make room for hers. Lifting her dress, Kane tugged it up to bunch around her waist. Her legs were covered in stockings with pale blue ribbons securing them on her thighs. Her drawers, however, were a hindrance.

Using both hands, Kane ripped the delicate material exposing the pale globes of her arse. He'd strategically placed her so I could get a good glimpse. He let the torn material fall to the wooden floor below her head so she could look at them. "No more drawers, baby. Your cunny must be available to us at all times. Spread your legs, please."

She shook her head in defiance.

Kane spanked her, his palm landing in a firm strike against her left cheek.

"Kane!"

She jolted and cried out more in surprise than in pain. The strike hadn't been overly hard; it was more of a warning and introduction than true punishment.

Quickly realizing Kane was very serious, she widened her legs and I could see her cunny clearly as Kane began to spank her. Even though I'd just come, my cock hardened at the sweet sight, her lips there red and swollen from being fucked twice. "Count, please."

Each strike landed someplace new on her untried bottom, the skin turning a light pink, yet quickly turning darker as she counted. It was the most arousing of sights. When she called out the tenth strike, she was crying, yet the fight had left her. Instead of kicking out and wiggling her hips, she'd given up and took her punishment, her body lax. Kane's strikes weren't overly hard, but solely for her to learn the consequences of her actions. She would be turned over a knee as needed, especially if she did something that would put her safety in jeopardy.

Seeing her accept the error of her ways was a sweet sight. Her submission was beautiful and I was very pleased. Kane, no doubt, was as well.

"Fifteen," she sobbed.

Gently, Kane caressed her hot flesh, soothing her with words. "You did beautifully, sweetheart, taking your punishment like a good girl."

Once she settled, her breaths coming evenly and slowly, Kane helped her up and onto the bench seat across from us once again, brushing the hair back from her face and kissing her brow gently. It was a mild spanking and she would quickly recover, however the hard seat and the bumpy ride would keep her mind on her transgression.

"Put yer feet up on our knees," I said.

She frowned at me in confusion, so I patted the bend in my leg where I intended. "Give me your foot." I held out my hands, palms up.

She lifted her foot and I placed it against the front of my knee. Once she saw what I expected, she placed the other one in Kane's hand and he placed it against his own knee. This position had her sitting lower on the bench so her arse was off the edge, keeping the brunt of her weight off her sore flesh.

"There. That's better, isn't it? Your arse will be sore for a little while, but sitting this way should ease your discomfort," I said, stroking my hand up and down her stocking covered calf.

It was also an unladylike position, her shoulders slumped, her legs wide, her breasts uncovered and thrust out. My smeared seed had dried upon them leaving a dappled haze on her creamy skin. Emma was most certainly a lady, but neither Kane nor I were gentleman, at least not when we were alone with her. "Pull your skirt up. Show me my cunny, or as ye say here in America, pussy."

When she didn't comply to my request, I arched my brow. Her eyes lowered and she complied, although her dislike of the action was obvious. Slowly, her fingers pulled the blue silk up higher and higher so it pooled at her waist. I moved my knee wider, which opened her legs further. We had the perfect vantage of her body.

"You are so beautiful, Emma. Every inch of you." I couldn't help but stare at her delectable cunny and the way the tops of her creamy thighs were at full advantage above the edge of her stockings.

Her cheeks heated and her hands gripped the edge of her seat, her knuckles white.

"Ye dinna ken so?" I asked.

She looked shocked by my question. "My breasts are exposed and my legs are apart and you can see...everything!"

Both of us grinned.

"Your body belongs to us and we will look at it as we wish. Your cunny is all swollen from our cocks, your lips there are open. Your arousal is obvious, lass. You doubt me, but your thighs, they're glistening with your desire. You liked the spanking."

She tried to move her legs together but I gripped her ankle, Kane the other. "I did not!" she replied, full of indignation.

"Your body doesn't lie, sweetheart," Kane said. "Your nipples are tight pink buds."

She pursed her lips, her eyes bright with anger.

"I allow ye to like it, lass," I told her, my voice soothing.

"Allow me?" Her voice dripped with sarcasm.

"Aye. Ye are allowed to enjoy showing your gorgeous

cunny to your men. Ye are allowed to be aroused by it, for we most certainly are. Touch yourself. Make yourself come."

"What?" she squeaked.

"Touch your cunny with your fingers until you come."

"I don't want to," she countered as she shook her head.

"Your mind dinna want to, but your body is desperate for release. As I said, I allow ye to like it. In fact, ye have nay choice. Ye will stay just like this until you come. I would assume we are close to Simms, which means the stage will stop."

"But the driver!" she cried.

We would never share the view of her delectable body with a stranger like the stage driver. Her body was precious. *She* was precious to us. "It's your choice. Show us how ye pleasure yourself or get another spanking beforehand."

She pulled against our hold on her ankles, but we would not release her. This was the time for her to learn to obey me. Both of us. Punishment would be plentiful because of her willful spirit, but she'd quickly learn that we always pleasured her when she was good.

"Five minutes to Simms! Five minutes," the stage driver yelled, his voice loud even over the rumbling of the wheels.

Emma gasped in surprise and her right hand flew to her cunny, her fingers rubbing over it in untried ways.

"Find your clit," Kane instructed. We wanted her to

succeed. She'd earned a sweet release. We wanted to watch her as she came for it was a most beautiful sight. "Remember that place I touched you yesterday with my fingers? Yes, I can see you found it. Now, small circles. Just like that."

We might force her to pleasure herself, but that didn't mean we couldn't guide her. She was inexperienced and it was our job to tell her what to do.

Her cunny was slippery and wet and soon her fingers were shiny and coated with her arousal. Her eyes fell closed and she relaxed into the seat, giving in to our demands and focusing on her cunny.

"Good girl. We can see what makes ye feel good. Oh, tiny circles on your clit? What about your cunny, your pussy, does it feel empty? Ye can slip your fingers of your other hand in, ye ken. Aye, like that." I talked to her all the while she played with herself. Her nipples softened, her back bowed and her mouth parted and I knew she was close. She was a glorious sight and perhaps we would have her sit on display like this every time we were in a stage.

"Come for us, lass. Show us your pleasure."

She shook her head back and forth, her hand continuing to move. "I can't, I can't do it!" she cried out.

Kane shifted, placing her foot on the edge of the bench seat and moved to sit beside her. He ran his hands over her puckered nipples and played with them as he leaned in and murmured in her ear. "Let go and come, baby. This isn't your decision. You don't have to like what you're doing, but you are allowed to feel pleasure in it. Feel pleasure knowing we are watching. You are so beautiful. Good girl."

Her body tensed and her eyes flared open in surprise. She cried out as she came, her back bowing, her fingers slipping over her clit persistently. Her skin flushed a pretty pink all the way down to her upturned breasts, her skin bright with a sheen of perspiration. When the tremors left her body, when her heart rate slowed, she remained slumped upon the seat, her eyes closed and a small smile on her lips. Her hand rested over her used cunny, her fingers glistening. We each held an ankle and enjoyed the view until the stage began to slow. There was nothing like a woman sated and replete from her pleasure, especially when the woman belonged to us.

CHAPTER SIX

EMMA

The ride from Simms to the men's ranch was several hours in duration. The exact length I was unsure of, but it felt interminable. I was sore...there, from the spanking, but also inside where my maidenhead used to be. They'd permitted me to button up the front of my dress so I appeared to the stage driver and any passerby that I was a modest, demure woman, although I now knew better.

Kane had insisted I ride upon his lap as it was horses only from Simms on. I'd objected at first, but he'd placed me sideways across his muscular thighs and the discomfort wasn't as terrible. He'd held me securely in the circle of his arms, the sway of the animal lulling me. I shouldn't have found comfort as I was, but I did.

The side of my face rested against his chest and I could hear the steady beat of his heart. He smelled good, radiated warmth and I felt...safe. With Ian riding beside us, I knew nothing could happen to me. Neither Thomas nor any other man would harm me again. And yet, was I safe from these men? They'd touched me, used me, punished me in ways I never imagined. It had all been so illicit, so carnal, so wrong. Everything I'd done in the stage was beyond my scope of imagination, but would probably be an everyday occurrence with them. The way they'd made me find pleasure in what I'd done had me confused, frightened even, by my own reactions. I'd liked it! Even after being so debased, I'd come, harder than any previous time and it had been incredibly *good.* All that had been missing was a cock filling me.

We rode up to a large house built solely of logs. It was two stories and vast, with a covered porch that wrapped all the way around. Ian tied his lead to a rail then came over and helped me down from Kane's lap. Various buildings were scattered about the land in the distance. A barn, with a hayloft was attached to a longer, one story stable. A fenced paddock with several horses grazing was beside it. Further away, several smaller structures, and in the distance, set upon rises in the landscape, were other houses, discernible by their porches, stone chimneys and windows. Our arrival must have been witnessed or heard as several men approached.

I smoothed out my dress as the men shook hands, caught up on the happenings at the ranch, too nervous to look any of them in the eye. Could they tell that I wore no drawers and had thick seed dried on my thighs? Would they know what Kane and Ian had forced me to do in the stage or that I had found my pleasure while doing so? I was certainly travel worn and unkempt, but would they associate part of that state to being on my knees servicing Ian or my head thrashing about as used my hand to make myself come?

All my concerns were irrelevant, as I quickly became the center of attention, completely surrounded by very large, very commanding men. There was something about their bearing that was identical – shoulders back, eyes assessing and sharp, bodies honed with muscle and strength. It was quite overwhelming. I glanced at Ian and Kane, whose looks included blatant possessiveness that I found surprisingly reassuring.

Kane moved to stand beside me and took my elbow, Ian did the same on the other side. "This is Emma, our bride."

With this pronouncement, the men's gazes shifted to scrutiny and I felt as naked and exposed as I had on the stage. My eyes widened, realizing that Kane had introduced me as *our bride.* Not his bride, not Ian's bride. Not one man seemed surprised. Had they missed his very specific wording?

"Emma, the bloke on the left is Mason." Kane indicated with his chin. "Next to him is Brody. Simon and Rhys are the dark-haired lads. You will discover as soon as they speak that they were members of our regiment as well. The last is Cross, who is as American as you are. We each own a stretch of land, but the ranch, Bridgewater, is our common goal."

I nodded my head and gave a smile, finally reassured I would not be taken to the other side of the world.

"Ann is expecting you two for the noon meal, although Emma will be quite a surprise." If I remembered correctly, it was Mason who spoke. He appeared a few years younger than both

Kane and Ian, with black hair and a neatly trimmed beard.

I tugged on Kane's sleeve and he leaned down. "Do they know...I mean–"

My whispered words were cut off by Ian. "They know ye belong to us. To ensure there is nay doubt, I'll repeat it for ye. Emma is our bride." The man puffed up with pride at the words and it felt very reassuring. "The men ken our ways, lass, because they share them as well. Ann is married to Robert and Andrew, who are off somewhere, but ye will meet them later."

My mouth fell open and stared at the large bunch of men before me. "You all, I mean, I belong to all of you?" I stepped back, eyes wide with fear. I felt the blood drain from my face. What had I gotten myself into? I couldn't handle all of these men. What was expected...?

"Emma," Kane's loud voice sliced through my thoughts. He grabbed my shoulders and lowered his head so his eyes held mine. "You belong to Ian and me. The other men, they will find their own wives."

"Wives?" I asked, licking my dry lips.

"Mason and Brody will claim a wife and Simon, Rhys and Cross another. In time."

He raised his brows as he watched me, asking without words if I understood. I nodded. "Ann? Does she know about–"

"As I said, she's married to Robert *and* Andrew. They are

the foremen here. Their house is over there." He pointed over my shoulder and I turned to see a house in the distance, set off on its own by a meandering creek. "There is nothing to worry about. Nothing to fear."

"We will ensure your safety."

I couldn't see who spoke as Kane blocked my view. He stood and Ian pulled me in for a hug, my cheek resting against his hard chest.

"There is no need to worry about anything but being our wife."

"You may belong to Kane and Ian, but you are one of us now. We will protect you as our own," another man added.

I didn't understand their ways. These weren't British ways, which I knew to be even more severe than in the American West; some other deeply rooted moral code was at work here. Their conviction for several of them to marry one woman was unusual, to say the least. But they believed it, were impassioned by it. They did not seem to sway, but held firm to this, and somehow, this set me at ease, at least somewhat so.

Kane kissed my hair. "There. Better?"

I nodded against his shirt quite relieved, yet completely overwhelmed.

KANE

One of the luxuries we added to the house when we built it was a water closet, complete with hip tub. We knew any woman would thrill in such a feature, especially during the harsh winter months. As we helped undress Emma and held her hand as she slipped into the warm water, just the look of sheer bliss on her face made all the effort worth it.

Sounds drifted up from downstairs as the noon meal was prepared, but we were far removed tending to Emma. She leaned against the high back, her hair swirling on the surface of the steaming water about her, her breasts bobbing on the surface and her pink nipples plump and lush. Ian glanced at me, his jaw clenching as he shifted his cock in his pants. I knew just how uncomfortable he felt. A hard cock would be a permanent state now.

We'd been gentle with her, but as a virgin, she did not have much chance to come to terms with her new role. Surely being married to two lusty men, living on a ranch with other men with similar leanings and notions, would require adjustment of mind. Her own story would need to be told, but not now, not when everything was so overwhelming. I wanted to know about her bastard step-brother, Thomas, so I could track him down and beat him bloody. He'd done her wrong. She wouldn't have ended up in Mrs. Pratt's auction otherwise. As her husbands, we'd ensure he never harmed Emma ever again. I was reassured knowing she was away from the man and safe at Bridgewater.

After her hair had been washed and her body cleaned, we helped her from the tub and dried her.

"I can do this all myself," she replied, trying to cover body.

"I assure you," I murmured as I rubbed her pink skin with a bath cloth. "This is no hardship."

"Come," Ian said, taking her hand and tugging her out into the hall.

"Ian, I'm naked!" She dug in her heels, but that was not enough resistance to stop the man. All it did was make her breasts sway and that only had me more intent than ever.

"Just the way I like you." He grinned at her over his shoulder. "You will have to learn to appreciate two men seeing how beautiful you are."

I grabbed the shaving supplies and a clean cloth and followed the duo into Ian's room. When I joined them, Emma was held within the firm hold of Ian's arms and they were kissing, his hands roaming up and down her back, then cupping the perfect globes of her arse. When finally he pulled back, Emma's eyes were dark like a stormy sea, her lips pink and swollen.

"I could do that all day, but we have things to do." He gave her one last peck on the lips. "Lay down, lass."

It wasn't hard for Ian to get her onto her back as the man's kiss seemed to have robbed her of all reasonable thought. Which was just the way we needed her for what we were about to do. Ian climbed onto the bed after her, moving so he leaned back against the pillows, pulling Emma up so she was lying against him. Her back to his front.

"Ian, what are you doing?" she asked, tilting her head to the side and glancing up at him. He took this opportunity to give her a lingering kiss.

"Ian is to hold you while I shave you," I told her.

Placing the shaving supplies on the side table, I grabbed the soapy brush and razor and sat down on the large bed as well.

"Shaving?" she asked, her brow furrowed.

Ian's hands slid down her body, taking a moment to cup and then play with her breasts before grabbing her inner thighs and pulling her knees up and back.

"Ian!" She tried to shift from his hold, but leaning against him as she was, she had no leverage.

"Shh," he soothed, kissing her ear and along her neck.

Ian did an excellent job of spreading her open for me, her knees up at the sides of her breasts. I shifted into position between her thighs and quickly began coating her in thick lather.

"I am shaving your cunny."

"Why?" she asked, confused and embarrassed. It was doubtful she realized she tilted her head to the side to give Ian better access to her long neck.

"Because your pretty pink lips are hidden beneath these dark curls and I want to feel every slick inch of you when I take you with my mouth." Placing the brush on the table, I picked up the razor. "Don't move now."

I tended to the task as Emma didn't move a muscle. Slipping my finger over the shaved area, it was so smooth, so slick to the touch.

"Kane? Ian?"

The shout came from downstairs. Mason. Most likely calling us to eat. I heard other footfall below, as the other men went to the dining room for the noon meal. The house was large, the dining area a distance from the bedrooms upstairs.

"We're up here," Ian called back.

Heavy footfalls made their way up the steps and I pulled the razor from between Emma's legs, stood and met the man at the door before he could enter. Mason stopped just outside the doorway, hat in hand, and took in the razor and cloth in my hands. My body blocked his view of Emma's very exposed body. It was for our eyes only, not Mason's or any other man's. His mouth quirked knowing what we were doing.

"Keep your bloody thoughts off our wife," I growled in possessiveness. Instead of wiping the small smile from his face, it only made him grin as he held up his hands in surrender.

"Sorry for interrupting, but I've got kitchen duty with Ann. We eat in ten minutes."

"Ian, let me go!" she whispered loudly. I knew Ian would not relent on his hold until we were done and we were far from it. Her resistance was futile.

I nodded at Mason, stepped back and shut the door in the man's face. I could hear his chuckle through the wood.

I turned to look at Emma, whose head was turned away from the doorway, her eyes closed. I moved back into position between her spread thighs.

"Don't move, baby." I went back to work, removing the last bits of dark hair from between her thighs, her pink, lush cunny more and more apparent with each stroke. "You are ours, baby. Only Ian and I will touch you. The men know what happens between men and their woman. They will know your pussy is being shaved. They will hear you when you come, for we will take you regularly and in places – albeit private ones – where you might be overheard. They may even hear you being spanked if warranted."

"But–"

"It is our job to train you to be our wife, to teach you what is expected. Becoming comfortable with others knowing how much you please us and are pleasured by us is something to which you must accustom."

"You *are* beautiful, lass," Ian said, his voice reassuring.

"I've been wondering what you taste like, baby." I glanced at Ian, then at Emma's wide-eyed stare. "I think I'll find out."

Shifting, I lowered my head between her thighs and licked her from arse to clit, my tongue feather light, only brushing over her newly exposed flesh.

"Kane!" she shouted, her eyes lowering to watch me. "What are you–"

Using my fingers, I spread her bare cunny lips, slick now with her cream. "Now doesn't that feel better?"

Her little pink pearl was hard and erect and begging for my tongue. Lapping away all of her arousal, my tongue flicked over her clit. Once. Twice. Her body jerked and she cried out.

"She tastes sweet. Like honey."

"She's fighting my hold," Ian added.

"You don't like your reward, Emma? You've been such a good girl. Stay still or you will be spanked."

I watched her from my position between her thighs. Her breathing made her flat belly rise and fall; her nipples were puffy pink tips, her skin was flushed. Long tendrils of damp hair clung to her forehead and neck. Her pale eyes were a misty blue, her emotions evident; arousal, fear, embarrassment.

"Is your cunny sore?" Ian whispered, her eyes falling shut as he licked the round shell of her ear. I heard a whimper escape her lips.

Carefully, I slipped a finger into her. She was slick and hot, her passage so very tight. My fingers only delved in about an inch, then pulled out and I added a second to the first. I watched her closely and when I slipped in to the second knuckle, her eyes opened and she winced slightly.

"Poor lass," Ian soothed. "Two big cocks took your maidenhead and stretched you wide. Your sore cunny needs time to heal, so instead of fucking you, we can start your training."

As he spoke, I returned to my task, flicking just the tip of my tongue over her clit. Her small hands pushed against Ian's thighs, trying to move away. She tasted sweet, tangy and her scent lifted from her heated skin to fill the air around us. My cock pulsed painfully against the placard of my pants. All it wanted to do was sink deep into her, sore cunny or not. I bloody hell wasn't going to hurt Emma with my baser needs so I took a deep breath, lowered my head and focused solely on my new wife's pleasure.

"Kane, it's...it's too much!"

My brow arched as I looked up her naked body. This was the first time a man's head was between her thighs and the pleasure would be different, perhaps even more intense than one of our cocks. "Am I hurting you?"

Her head thrashed. "No." She swallowed.

"Then I will continue, for I wish to see you come." And I did, lapping at her, sucking on her little nub, nipping it gently with my teeth.

"No, please. I don't like this!" she cried out.

I didn't stop as Ian asked her, "It doesn't feel good?" His hands cupped her breasts once again, played with them.

She sighed as I flicked her clit just right. The little nub was hard and very sensitive against the tip of my tongue. "Yes, but–"

"You don't want to come?"

"Not...no, I can't like it!" Her damp hair clung to the sides of her face, in long tendrils over Ian's chest.

I didn't stop, only added a finger to just the very opening of her cunny, letting it move in the smallest of circles, around and around. I loved having her hairless here. So smooth, so pink. Luscious.

"Why not, lass?" Ian murmured as he kissed the thrumming pulse at her neck.

"Because...there's two of you."

I lifted my head from between her luscious thighs. Her inner walls were greedily squeezing at the tip of my finger, trying to pull it in. Her clit had grown bigger and harder beneath my tongue, her cream slipping from her to coat my chin. There was no question she was about to come, but her mind was too diverted by the morality of it all. This was a barrier we would break through, just like I had her maidenhead. It would take time, but it was one of the most important aspects being married to Ian and I. She would accustom herself to being pleasured by both of us. Together.

Because of this, I slowly wiped the back of my hand across my chin. "Then I will stop."

Her eyes opened and met mine, her body still. "What?" she asked, now more confused than ever.

"If you do not wish to come, then I will stop," I repeated, moving off the bed. My cock was hard as a rock, but tending to it would have to wait.

Ian released her legs and she sat up, confusion warring with arousal on her face. She had no idea how pretty she was with her hair damp and down her back, long tangles of curl fell over her shoulder and onto an upturned breast. Her skin was flushed and the way she sat, her legs curled, her bare cunny was exposed. The swollen pink folds couldn't be missed.

Shifting from behind her, Ian moved from the bed to his dresser and took a small box that held handcrafted butt plugs. Opening it, he took the smallest size from the selection along with a small glass jar of slick lubricant. I had the honor of taking her virginity and the first to sample the sweetness between her thighs. Therefore, it was Ian's turn to work her body, teaching Emma we would both tend to her, one at a time, for now.

Ian sat on the edge of the bed. "Over my knee, lass."

Her eyes widened and she dashed off the far side of the bed, pressing her back against the wall. In this position, she only showcased her assets for us even more. I was reveling in her bare cunny and just stared at it while Ian took over. I leaned against the doorway, relaxed and ready to watch what came next. Just looking at her all mussed and naked had me adjusting my hard length in my pants.

"You're not spanking me. I've done nothing wrong!"

"Nay, lass. You've behaved so well. I want ye over my knee so I can begin your arse training, not to spank ye."

"My...what?" Her eyes were wide, her mouth open.

"We Scots – Brits, too, like Kane – say arse, but you can say ass instead. Say it, lass." When she didn't Ian's eyebrow went up, all but daring her to be contrary.

"Ass," she whispered, looking down at her toes.

"Very good. Now come over here." His tone dropped an octave.

Emma glanced at both of us, considering her options, the consequences. She was a smart woman, well educated; I didn't need to *know* her to recognize a well-bred woman. Moving slowly, her bare feet silent on the wood floor, she came around the bed to stand before Ian.

He cupped the nape of her neck and pulled her into a kiss. I pushed off the wall to stand directly behind her, my cock nudging against the small of her back. Lowering my head, I kissed her bare shoulder, sliding her curtain of hair out of the way, slipped my hands up and down her arms. Just because she didn't want to come didn't mean we were strong enough to keep our hands from her.

As soon as Ian ended their kiss, I returned to my place against the wall. Ian tugged, pulling her across his lap, her upper body on the bed beside him, as she gasped in surprise.

"Ian!" Pushing up on her elbows, she turned and looked over her shoulder, fire swirling from the blue depths of her eyes. Ian's large palm rested at her lower back, ensuring she could not rise.

Ian dipped two of his fingers into the jar of ointment, coating them with the clear, greasy substance.

"I could kiss ye all night. There's nay chance I will ever tire of your taste, but I want to claim your arse," Ian told her. "We will fuck your there, frequently, but you are not ready yet. Dinna fash," he replied in a soothing tone when she began to squirm. "We don't want to hurt you and it is our job to get you ready. To train your arse to take our cocks."

When his fingers ran over the pink pucker, she bucked and thrashed. "No. This isn't right."

"It is right." As he spoke, Ian circled his fingers over her, slowly pressing inward. "Serving your husbands, pleasing them, is a wife's job. Ye will serve us by offering all of your holes. Your tight pussy, your delectable mouth and your snug arse. It will bring us pleasure for ye to do so and in return, we will give you the most incredible pleasure. We took your cunny and ye loved it. Ye had your first lesson in sucking cock earlier and ye came after. Now, we must ready your arse."

Her body stiffened and she groaned when one of Ian's fingers slipped past the tight ring inside her snug arse. She'd fought valiantly, but her body would offer no contest to our attentions. We would show her all the way, all the places pleasure could be found. She may be wary now, but she would soon love having us play with her arse. That thought had my cock pulsing, throbbing with the need to claim her there. But she wasn't ready and her submission to Ian would be satisfaction enough. For now. Soon, she would trust us, knowing that we would see her happy, sated and well satisfied at every turn.

"We dinna want to hurt you, lass. We're doing this for ye." Ian slowly worked his finger in and out of her arse, Emma's body slumped across his lap, her breathing erratic and loud. As he moved further and further within, she mewled, little sounds escaping the back of her throat.

"Our friend Rhys is quite skilled at carpentry, including the lathe. He handcrafts all of the dildos and butt plugs for us, ye ken? When Andrew and Robert married Ann, he made some to their specifications. Even though we hadn't met ye yet, Ian and I knew what we wanted to train our wife. Rhys made them for us and we've kept them, waiting. Waiting for just this moment. Dinna fash, I will use the smallest size plug."

I couldn't resist any longer, moving to kneel on the floor by her hip. Moving my hand beneath Ian's I slipped my fingers over her pussy lips. "She's dripping wet," I commented seeing her slick pussy lips and thighs. My words elicited another moan from her.

"Do you like this, lass?" Ian asked.

She shook her head but said nothing.

"Your body tells us otherwise, lass. Can you feel all the secret places in your arse awakening to my touch? Kane can feel how slick ye are now. Both of your men's hands are on ye, lass. Poor baby, so needy."

Carefully, Ian slowly worked his second finger in to join the first, slowly fucking her, stretching her open as I easily found her clit, hard and eager for my touch.

"No." Her breath was escaping in little pants. "I...I don't like this."

"What? That you feel pleasure in my touching you here? That Kane is watching your arse be stretched for the first time? That he's playing with your clit?"

She shifted her hips back, not realizing she wanted his fingers deeper, perhaps mine as well. When Ian filled her even further, she began to cry. Not in pain, most certainly not. We would never touch her and cause harm. This was the antithesis of her feelings. She needed to come so much that she was falling into a depth of frustration that had her overwhelming emotions escape through tears instead of release. "This is wrong!"

Using his free hand, Ian picked up the small plug Rhys had

so expertly crafted, dipped it into the jar so that it was thickly coated, then gently pulled his fingers free, her body slumping into his lap. The way her body clenched down upon Ian's digits, I imagined the strangling grip her body would have on my cock. I stifled a groan as my cock swelled even further.

Before he nudged the plug up to the opening, I could see her opening wink once as it closed back up. Ian didn't offer her body the chance to do so, moving the slippery plug within in a slow, smooth stroke. She groaned and her entire muscles tensed once again, so I ran my hand up and down her leg in an attempt to soothe her.

Settled in place, the dark wooden handle could be readily seen, protruding only a small bit. She was stretched open slightly, just a start for her to begin adjusting in preparation for our cocks. Her swollen and aroused cunny lips beneath my fingers were hot and slippery. I'd set her body ablaze from putting my mouth upon her just a few minutes earlier. Although she hadn't wanted her arse played with, there was no missing how it had intensified her pleasure, her need to come. Her thighs were slick with her honey and her skin was coated in a sheen of perspiration. Moving my hand down, I flicked her clit and Emma arched her back, crying out.

She sobbed, a sound of need escaping from within that ripped at my control.

"See, baby? Only pleasure," I told her, continuing to stroke her cunny and her leg.

"You may come, lass."

I nudged her clit again when she didn't respond right away.

Sniffling, she said, "I...I don't want that thing in me. It's too big."

She was still focusing on what we were doing to her instead of how she felt.

"Not as big as either of our cocks, Emma," I reminded. We will fuck you at the same time, baby, Ian in your arse while I fill your cunny."

"How...how is that possible?" she asked, breathless.

"It's possible, lass. More than possible. It *will* happen," Ian said.

She groaned, probably envisioning how much more she'd be filled when we finally fucked her.

"You've done beautifully. Come now for us. Let us see. Show us you're such a good girl," Ian prompted.

"No," she sniffed. "No. I can't. Oh God."

She was so desperate, so lost. We were letting her decide if she would come, instead of commanding. It was clear she would need to be told to come, to take the decision to cede to the pleasure away from her. She wanted to submit. If Ian changed his tone, his wording ever so slightly to be less soothing and more demanding, Emma most likely would go off like a Fourth of July firecracker.

It was blatant how inhibited she was. How much her brain was in control of her body. And so another lesson would be taught today. With her answer, Ian carefully and slowly pulled the plug from her arse and we helped her stand, keeping his hold on her until she gained her bearings. We would have kept the plug in longer as part of her training, but she needed to learn that playing with her arse was going to be pleasurable, not embarrassing. It would make her come – we would ensure it – and she was denying herself that release. Both of us had our hands on her intimately, working her, yet still she refused. Therefore, we would give her what she wished. Soon enough, she'd *want* us to touch her there. To be touched by both of us at the same time. Until she recognized that, she'd remain on edge.

I stood. "Let's get you dressed. Everyone will wonder what we've been up to."

It was very hard not to smile at the look on Emma's face. She was so aroused her blue eyes were foggy, blurry with her need. Her mouth was open and she breathed in little pants. A pink flush brightened her cheeks and crept down her neck and to the tops of her breasts. A brighter pink tinged her plump nipples and she squeezed her slick thighs together. "But...."

Ian put a finger over her lips. "Shh. Ye did not wish to come and that is fine. We will always give ye pleasure, lass, ye only have to accept it. It is time to eat."

She frowned, her smooth brow marred with a crinkle of confusion.

Ian left to go into the washroom and return with her blue dress. He lowered it to the floor and I helped Emma step in, put her arms through the sleeves and began to do the long line of buttons up the front.

"As we said in the stage, no drawers for you. It will be quite uncomfortable for me to sit at dinner with a raging cock know your pussy is shaved and bare."

"Aye," Ian agreed.

"This dress is temporary until after the meal when we can ask Ann for some clothes. You are both of similar size and her dresses may work for you in the short term, perhaps with some sewing adjustments."

As I did up the buttons over her breasts, the sides of my hands brushed at her sensitive nipples and a sigh escaped her lips. She would quickly learn that her pleasure came before propriety while here on the ranch. Until she asked to come – begged for it – she would be in quite a state. And so would Ian and I.

CHAPTER SEVEN

EMMA

The evening meal was not a small affair. Even though the house belonged to Kane and Ian, the dining room was large, the vast table able to seat up to twenty. All of the men I'd met earlier were seated around it and stood at my entrance along with a few new faces, including one woman.

"I am Ann," she said. "It will be very nice to have another woman about." She was perhaps a few years older than me, with a broad smile and a soft demeanor. Her hair was a pale wheat color, pulled back neatly into a bun at her nape. With pale skin and blue eyes, she was quite striking. As Kane had said, we were similar in size, although my bosom was much more ample than her more dainty curves. In my tawdry blue dress with my hair a wild tangle down my back, I looked as wanton as I felt.

I forced a smile to my lips, but it was difficult, knowing everyone in the room was aware of the reasons for our tardiness. If they didn't, seeing me in such a fashion would provide answer enough. My cheeks were red, I could feel the heat, and my nipples were tight little buds beneath the fabric and there was no corset to hide that fact.

My pussy, my cunny as Kane and Ian called it, throbbed and

pulsed with unrequited need. It felt...strange being shaved. Smooth and noticeably slick. My bottom was sore from Ian's fingers and the hard plug, but it, too, pulsed and little sparks of pleasure erupted every time I clenched down.

Ian pulled out a chair for me and I sat without thought, my husbands sitting on either side of me. "That is Robert and Andrew, Ann's husbands," Kane said, pointing to two men who smiled and nodded at me from across the table. All the men on this ranch were large, as if the fresh air, hard work and good food made them this way.

The plates and bowls of food were passed around the table, Kane or Ian filling my plate as they came by. I was thankful they were assisting me with this nominal task, for my thoughts were too scattered, yet at the same time too focused on my body and the craving I felt for release.

"The men have houses of their own, but we eat our meals together," Kane continued. He acted as if nothing had happened upstairs just minutes before, although he did say his cock was hard. Perhaps he was just better at hiding his need than I. "Ann will come in the morning to cook along with one of the men, the role rotating daily so she has help. You can offer your help as well, or if you are inclined or skilled, in some other part of the ranch."

I picked at the food on my plate, listening to Kane's words, but focused solely on my body. I couldn't help squeezing my thighs together to lessen the ache, although it didn't seem to help. I was sore, not only from my maidenhead being torn, but from Ian working my bottom. I squirmed on the hard seat trying to attain relief. Nothing seemed to help. I feared the only solution was what the men had offered not once, but twice – sweet release. I needed to come.

"Eat, lass." Ian leaned in and kissed my brow, then returned to his food.

"Are you all right?" Ann asked, seated across from me. She tilted her head and studied me. "You look feverish. Was your journey too arduous?"

I shook my head, having no interest in revealing *why* I looked overheated.

"As you might remember from your first day or two as a bride, Ann, Emma is tending to the needs of two very ardent men." It was either Robert or Andrew who spoke. I couldn't remember which one had the beard and which had blond hair.

Awareness lit the other woman's face. "It's not too terrible, is it?" Ann asked, biting her lip. Her eyes darted to her husband beside her.

"Terrible?" her husband queried. "If I remember correctly, Kane came running because he thought you were being beaten, when you were actually screaming your pleasure."

Kane chuckled. "I remember that quite well."

"Do you remember *why* you came so hard that time?"

Ann blushed to the roots of her blond hair. "I...I can't say."

"It was the first time we stretched your ass. You found it most enjoyable."

"Robert," Ann chided, looking down at her untouched meal. She shifted in her seat.

"I know it is hard for you to voice how you please us, but it is something you need to practice. If you won't tell her about your pleasure, then you will tell her about your punishments." Andrew's voice, although patient and calm, was deep. Neither man had British accents.

"But...I don't want to tell anyone about that."

"There's no shame in making amends. You can tell her about a punishment or she can watch one firsthand." I recognized Andrew's stern tone as both Kane and Ian had used it with me.

"I am spanked," she replied, squirming. The reply was short and met her husband's request, but by the frown on both her husbands' faces that was not the answer they expected.

"Emma has most likely learned about that punishment by now," Robert replied. "Give her a reason for why you were spanked, please."

Ann licked her lips. "I went near the stallion in the outer pen."

I was an accomplished rider, but I did not know how dire her act was.

Andrew clarified for me. "The stallion sensed the mare was in heat and was solely focused on mounting her. Ann did not heed our warnings for her safety and neared the primed animal."

It did sound dangerous.

"Ann is the most precious thing in the world and we can not keep her safe if she disregards any of the ranch rules." Robert ran a knuckle down Ann's cheek. She turned her face and smiled lovingly at Robert. Andrew stroked down her pale hair and she turned her gaze to him next.

Their love was blatant and being punished did not seem to hinder their relationship. Ian and Kane, while stern and clearly willing to guide me to their expectations, did not hold grudges regarding my transgressions either. Once a punishment was meted, all was forgiven. I did not have to worry that they would consider me an unworthy bride – quite the opposite, in fact. They seemed rather pleased with me. It was I who struggled with the arrangement.

The other men around the table ate their meals like men half starved. Utensils scraped across the china as they cleaned their plates, grabbing bowls and platters for additional helpings. But there was no question they followed the conversation.

"Stop squirming, sweetheart," Andrew said to Ann.

"I'm sorry, but it's–" She leaned in and whispered in his ear.

"It pleases us to know you have a plug in your ass. In fact, pleased is not the right word. You are not the only one uncomfortable at the table."

Confusion marred Ann's face and Andrew took the fork from her hand and placed it on her plate, then lowered her hand to his lap. "Oh!" she cried.

Both her husbands were looking upon Ann with very heated, very aroused gazes.

Kane leaned his head toward mine. I noticed his clean, male scent. Soap and something else I didn't recognize, but it was intoxicating. I clenched my thighs together. "As you can see, Ian and I are not the only ones with hard cocks."

I did feel some satisfaction in knowing my men were as aroused as I. "To what are they referring?" I asked.

"She has a plug in her ass."

My eyes widened thinking about having my bottom opened and stretched as it had been earlier during a meal. In public.

"Ye wonder why she has a plug inside her now, at dinner?" Ian leaned in and whispered.

It was as if he could read my mind. I gave a small, curt nod.

"In time, you will keep a plug in your arse for longer durations so that you are able to take a cock, to take both of us at the same time," Kane told me. "Stretching you, filling you with the plug for a few minutes was just a start."

"Surely not at dinner?" I squeaked.

Ian shrugged casually. "We will have to see, ye ken, and before ye say anything further, it is nay your decision."

"We will decide what's best for you," Kane added. "Just like Robert and Andrew decide for Ann."

"It's best to have a...plug in me?"

"To take a cock in your arse, for both of us to take you at the same time, yes. We do not wish to hurt you and will only claim that delectable hole of yours when you are truly prepared," Kane said, cutting his steak. This conversation was preposterous; talking about plugs and bottoms over a meal was unfathomable. Until now.

"Prepared and aroused," Ian added.

I gulped at the thought, remembering the size of their cocks, how big they'd felt when they'd fucked me. How good it had been. They wanted to put them...there? One in my bottom and one in my pussy, at the same time? What had I gotten myself into? And why, *why* was the idea of them taking me in such a way only adding to the need they'd aroused in me?

"Ann enjoys it when we fuck her ass, which we do frequently," one of her husbands said. "We are very careful with her, ensuring she is ready for us. She needs a maintenance plug so that she is stretched enough to take us."

"We are doing it for her," the other added. "Everything we do is for Ann."

"This entire conversation is an odd choice for dinner," I commented. "Odd in general."

"Weren't expecting two husbands?" Rhys asked. I looked down the table at the dark haired man.

"Certainly not," I replied.

"Assumed ye'd be fucked beneath the covers with the lamp extinguished?" Ian asked, light eyebrow raised.

I could feel my cheeks heat. "That is what I'd heard," I replied. I thought of Thomas and Allen and Clara and they'd certainly provided an alternative to a bed. What I'd had to do for my husbands in the stage had also altered my perspective.

"Perhaps, baby, what you heard wasn't normal," Kane said, placing his hand on top of mine and offering a light squeeze. "Perhaps what we do here at Bridgewater *is* normal."

I frowned. "What is normal then?"

"Normal is whatever a husband wishes. Whatever pleases a wife. It could be straight fucking."

"It could be arse fucking," Ian added.

"Ass play," Andrew said.

"Cock sucking."

"Eating pussy."

"Anywhere."

"Everywhere."

The men all added something else to the carnal conversation until my mind was filled with an abundance of variation I never knew were possible.

"Pleasing both your husbands," Ann said. Andrew and Robert turned to her, Andrew tilting her face up to him so he could kiss her, then Robert had his turn.

"See, lass, there is nay need to be embarrassed," Ian said reassuringly. "Ye only need to be aroused. What we did with ye earlier, starting your ass training–"

"Tasting your delectable pussy," Kane cut in.

"–is all for your pleasure. And you denied yourself release."

"Emma, heed these words from another woman," Ann said, leaning forward. "If your men are offering you pleasure. Take it. Accept it. *Enjoy* it." She grinned.

Shifting in my seat, I realized I ached between my thighs, and not because both men had claimed me. No, it was the pulsing of that little bundle of nerves I'd rubbed and touched until I screamed while riding the stage, where Kane had licked and sucked. Upstairs, they'd left me needy, because I'd asked them to. I longed now for them to touch me, knowing it was the only way for this ache to go away. My nipples had tightened beneath my dress, hardening at my wandering thoughts. As Ann said, I had to accept it and I'd most assuredly enjoy it."

"There were men over in Bozeman asking questions," one of the men said, thankfully changing the course of conversation.

I didn't remember his name, but he had dark hair with equally dark eyes.

Everyone stopped eating and the room fell silent.

"How did ye hear about this, Simon?" Ian asked, his tone grim.

"I was in town when you were gone and Taylor at the saloon was blabbering."

"So you got him drunk," Mason surmised.

Simon nodded. "Pulled him into a game of cards. Nothing he said about the men should have piqued my interest, but he mentioned they had funny accents. His words, not mine."

This group of men was the one with the funny accents, but discovering there was another – or a few men – that spoke in a similar fashion, especially in the Montana Territory, would be memorable.

"It was only a matter of time," Ian said, giving a disappointed shake to his head.

"It's been five years," Mason countered, pointing a fork at Ian.

"Evers won't give up."

When the men returned to their food, it seemed the conversation was over. I turned to Ian. "Who is Evers?"

He looked at me and smiled, little crinkles forming at the

corner of his eyes. Even in the brief time I'd known him, I could tell the smile was forced, that he was trying to protect me. He wanted me to be burden free. "Just someone we all used to work with. In the army."

"In England?" I asked.

"Mohamir."

Mohamir? "Is that near Persia?" I asked.

Kane nodded. I looked his way. "Yes."

The men finished their food without any more discussion, all clearly quiet in their thoughts. It seemed I was to be kept from the details regarding something that involved them years before. None wished to delve into conversation about it, but it seemed to have affected all of their spirits. Finished with their meal, they stood and cleared the table, carrying all of the dishes into the kitchen to be washed. It appeared Mason was the dishwasher tonight as well as cook's helper; from what was said earlier, they must rotate this task as well. I blushed at how he'd come to the bedroom door earlier and how, at the time, my legs had been pinned back by Ian as Kane shaved me. Fortunately, Kane had kept the man from seeing me naked and lewdly exposed, but he most assuredly knew what the men had done. My cheeks burned.

When Mason caught me looking at him, he gave me a smile and winked. I flushed even hotter and turned away. As I stood in the center of the kitchen, the men swirled around me and I felt overwhelmed. Everyone was so familiar with each other, so organized, so at ease. I felt out of place, on edge and wary of any misstep. Instead of remaining in the throng, I decided I could help by picking up any remaining dishes, so I returned to the dining room only to stop in my tracks just inside the doorway.

In the corner was Ann, hands on the wall, Robert close behind her. Fucking her. Naive as I was, I knew what I was witnessing, although I never knew it was possible to do standing up. Robert's pants were open enough only to free his cock, which from across the room, was quite large. He buried it all the way into Ann, then pulled back, his hands on her hips, pulling them back and keeping her in place, filling her again and again.

Andrew stood beside her, his cock out and his hand stroking up and down. "Good girl, Ann. Neither of us could wait to fuck you as we watched you shift and squirm in your chair knowing your ass was nice and filled, knowing you belong to us."

His words weren't harsh, but kind, pleasing. Soothing. Ann cried out, and most definitely in pleasure. "Yes, oh, Robert. Harder."

"Do ye like what ye see?"

The words at my ear had me jump, my hand flying to my chest. "Ian, you scared me."

"You may think Andrew and Robert are harsh men, perhaps cruel to speak so frankly about Ann. Do they look uncaring to you?"

Ann came right then, her sign of pleasure escaping as a deep moan.

The sound shook me to my core. I wanted to have the attention of my husbands just like Ann did right now. I wanted to feel what Ann was, a bone deep pleasure that couldn't be dampened. I shifted, rubbing my thighs together, which were now decidedly wet. My nipples tightened almost painfully.

"See? They cherish Ann, just as we cherish you."

"Why are they doing this where we can witness?"

"They are taking care of her. You saw that Andrew was aroused at the table. None of them could wait. She needs her men to recognize when she is ready for a good fucking. Most of that squirming she did at dinner wasn't because of the plug, but because her cunny was ready to be fucked. Her needs come first, wherever they are. All of us understand this. Besides, Ann knows how pleased her husbands are with her and they are not afraid to show it."

Andrew thrust one last time, held himself deep as he clenched his jaw, his grip tightening on Ann's hips. After a moment, he pulled out, his cock now replete, white seed dripping from Ann beneath a dark object that protruded from her back entrance. Oh! That was the plug? It looked so big! They could take her with that within her?

Robert took Andrew's spot behind Ann and without ceremony, filled her up. "Ann, you're so tight, so slick with seed."

Ian took my hand and pulled me from the room and toward the stairs as Ann's moans followed us. "Where are we going?"

Kane was waiting for us on the landing. "You've pleased us this meal, so we are tending to you."

CHAPTER EIGHT

KANE

Simon's words over dinner had me distracted and agitated. Downright mad. I was leading my wife up to my bedroom to strip her naked and make her scream and I was thinking about the men that were coming for Ian. There was no question it was Evers, or at least men sent by Evers. Once they found Ian, they'd drag him back to England for trial. Or, they'd drag him just over the ridge and shoot him, their own kind of vigilante justice. None of us would let that happen. Ian had done no wrong and Evers knew it. But pinning his own dastardly crimes onto Ian had kept the man in good standing. A duke could not be sullied by the dirtiness of murder, even in wartime. Even in a land, a culture, so different as Mohamir.

As Ian closed the door behind us with a definitive click, I had to put those thoughts away for now. Emma needed our attention. Deserved it. Required it. When Ian's eyes met mine over her head, I could read his thoughts. Whatever happened to him, I would take care of our wife. I would be here for her. Protect her. Even when Ian was gone.

Like bloody hell.

The sun had dipped lower, the room filled with soft evening

light, but not dark enough yet to require the lamp. A soft breeze came in through the open window and I could hear the men still working downstairs. Once the cleanup was complete, they'd finish up any remaining chores with the horses and return to their own homes spread out across the ranch.

"Have ye seen a man fully naked before, Emma?" Ian asked, undoing the buttons of his shirt.

She shook her head, keeping a careful watch on Ian's fingers, the expanse of chest exposed one button at a time.

"I was naked but I fucked her beneath the covers at the hotel this morn," Ian told Kane, then grinned sheepishly. "We were short on time."

"You won't be fucked under the covers again until the next blizzard. Your arousal has been taunting me the entire meal."

"My...my arousal?"

"The scent of you. Your hard nipples poking against your dress. Your flushed cheeks. Take off your dress, baby," I said, my voice rough. I'd had to will my cock into submission earlier when I had my face between her thighs, when I'd watched Ian work the plug into her virgin ass. Even through dinner. Now, though, I couldn't wait any longer.

"Doesn't it bother you that Mason knows what we were doing earlier? Shouldn't Andrew and Robert keep what they do with Ann a secret?" she asked, unbuttoning her bodice. I didn't mind the question, just thankful she was taking off her dress without duress.

I paused in my undressing and gave her my full attention as it was a serious question. An important one.

"There are no secrets at Bridgewater, baby."

"Privacy, yes, but nay secrets," Ian added.

"None of the other men will covet you as we do if they know your pussy is shaved and perfectly smooth. They will not think less of you if they hear your screams when you come. In fact, they will be right angry with us if they don't know you're being well tended. Your pleasure only validates our being good husbands."

"Ye belong to us and they ken that," Ian added. "Just as Ann belongs to Andrew and Robert even though we saw them fuck her downstairs. The other men will soon find brides of their own soon enough."

She considered our words as she stood there, her bodice open wide enough to glimpse the creamy swells of her breasts. I needed to calm myself; I wanted to relieve all the tension in my body by getting lost in hers. But that was not going to happen tonight. Her cunny was sore and not an option for relief, however there were many possible other ways to please her, and have her please us in return.

She fumbled with the remaining buttons, distracted by Ian and most definitely still aroused from earlier. We'd left her needy and wanting, her orgasm so close yet unattainable. Only when she accepted the pleasure as her due as our wife would we let her come. It was a self-inflicted punishment all in itself.

"Why does this man Evers anger you?" she asked. I must have answered her previous question readily enough for her to change topics. It did not seem to be in her nature to leave any worries unresolved.

Ian paused as he undid the placket of his pants, frowned. "He was our commanding officer during our time in the Mohamir."

"Our?"

"Don't stop, Emma. I want to see you," I told her, redirecting her thoughts. Her fingers began to move once again, but I could tell by the focused look in her gorgeous eyes that she wasn't to be deterred. I wanted to know her thoughts, share her experiences, learn about her. Evers was just someone neither of us wanted to think about, let alone talk about, especially when a hint of pink nipple appeared as the loose dress started to slip off her shoulder.

"Kane and I. Mason, Brody, Simon and Rhys, too." Ian said the last man's name with the English pronunciation, “Reese.” "We were stationed together to guard the British ships in the Dardanelles for a time, then travelled with British dignitaries to Mohamir to meet the religious and secular leaders of the region."

The dress slipped from her body and pooled around her feet.

Both Ian and I paused and looked our fill, watching as her nipples tightened. It seemed I had a slight obsession with her nipples.

I yanked at my shirt, stripping myself of my clothes as quickly as possible. Ian was already naked and positioned himself in the middle of the bed. "Come to me, lass."

Emma climbed onto the bed and Ian tugged her across his chest, kissing her, his arms wrapping around her securely. My mouth watered with my need to kiss her as well. It had been too long. An hour, perhaps?

"Evers doesn't matter now," Ian said, lifting his head to look at her, to stroke her hair back from her face. "Christ, you're so wet I can feel it on my thigh." He lifted his leg up so it pushed against her bare cunny.

Going around the bed, I sat with my back against the footboard, watching, lifting one hand to caress over the long line of her leg.

"Since you're too sore to fuck, I'm going to taste ye. Up ye go," Ian said, lifting Emma easily and turning her around so she faced me, but still across Ian's body on all fours. Grabbing her hips, he pulled her back so she was astride his face.

"Ian, what–"

I knew the moment Ian started to lick and suck at her cunny when her eyes widened and she startled, her breasts swaying beneath her as she did so.

"She's so smooth, so bloody slick. She tastes incredible," Ian murmured from between her thighs.

"Do you want to come, Emma?" I asked her. Her eyes had fallen shut and she was gasping at every expert flick of Ian's tongue.

"Yes!" she cried out.

"You're not worried about it being wrong?" I asked, intentionally prodding her. We'd left her unfulfilled earlier because she considered it wrong to find pleasure in being with both of us, in having us touch her body. *All* of her body in various, very intimate, ways. I hoped not to continue with this lesson, but would if required.

She shook her head, her dark hair a curtain around her shoulders, down her back.

"No? Before dinner you didn't want to come."

"I...I need it."

I smiled at her, although she couldn't see me with her eyes squeezed shut.

"Good girl. Look down, Emma."

Her eyes fluttered open to glance down at Ian's erect cock, just an inch from her chin. "Suck him, baby." I shifted so that my cock was just to her right. "Suck both of us. After you swallow our seed, Ian will make you come."

I could tell Ian slowed his attentions because Emma shifted

her hips and mewled.

"Take him into your mouth, just like you learned in the stage."

She did, working Ian with little licks, then taking him into her mouth as far as she could. He was big, too big for her now.

"Put your hand around the base, lean your forearm on the bed. Yes, like that. Now, use your other hand on me. Good girl."

It didn't take Ian long to come; he was no doubt as ready as I. Watching Emma take the plug earlier then seeing her watch another woman get fucked had been my personal torture. The look on her face, the unvarnished need, had had me on the brink of coming in my pants like a randy teenager. Seeing her ride Ian's face wasn't helping matters. Licking up every luscious drop of her honey most certainly pushed him over the edge. I remembered how sweet she tasted from earlier.

His hips thrust up and he groaned. Emma's cheeks hollowed, sucking him, taking his seed, her throat working to accommodate it all. She lifted her head and wiped her mouth with the back of her hand, only a small drop of seed on her lip.

"Good girl, baby. You took it all. Take my seed now and Ian will give you your reward."

Her face was flushed, her eyes half lidded with desire. Lower, her nipples were a bright pink and tightly furled.

"You want your reward?"

She nodded. "Oh yes," she said breathily, turning her head and opening her red, swollen lips to take me deep.

I hissed out my breath at the heat of her mouth, how wet it was, how her tongue stroked over the thick vein along my length. My balls drew up readying for my release.

"There's nothing wrong, baby, with getting pleasure from your husbands," I gritted out through clenched teeth. "Giving it to us. Yes, just like that, now suck. Good girl." I couldn't talk for a minute, watching her head bob in my lap, feel the tight suction of her drawn cheeks. The pleasure was so intense I was on the brink of spurting into her throat.

With Ian recovered, he returned to fervently work Emma's cunny, gripping her hips firmly to hold her in place. As she sucked me, she moaned, sending delicious vibrations up the length of my cock. They were my undoing. Nothing could stop the orgasm from coming and I groaned. As I did so, she too came, screaming around my cock, swallowing my seed voraciously, her hands clenching into fists in the quilt. Once I stopped pulsing in her mouth, she lifted her head and cried out. "Ian, yes!"

Ian flipped their positions so Emma rested on her back and we both began working her. She'd come once, but we weren't done. My hand delved to the juncture of her thighs finding her slick and wet, easily, yet gently, slipping two fingers into her tight channel. I set about to discover her secret pleasure spots, finding that little ridge of flesh inside that made her cry out, as

Ian sucked on one nipple, pulling and tugging with his teeth, his fingers working the other.

Emma came again quickly, her body arching like a bow, a rough scream escaping her lips. Ian grabbed the jar of lubricant and dipped his fingers in as I flipped Emma over once again. This time, Ian worked a finger into her tight arse as I continued to fuck her cunny with my fingers. As we did so, we spoke to her. *Ye are so bloody beautiful, Emma. You're so sensitive, look how you're coming again. See, you can come with something in your arse. Oh, it's so much better, isn't it? Soon it will be our cocks filling you. Together.*

We worked her until her voice was hoarse, her skin coated in sweat, her body mindlessly riding our fingers until she wilted in complete exhaustion.

With her on her stomach as she was, Ian retrieved the small plug we'd used on her earlier. Slick from his fingers, the plug was able to slip in easily. She didn't even stir. We admired how pretty her cunny was, especially knowing her arse was stretching in preparation for us taking her together. Pulling her beneath the covers, we let her sleep and I was more than pleased with the progress she was making. Thrilled we'd saved her from an uncertain fate. Touched that she belonged to us.

***

"Who's going with you?" I asked Ian from the kitchen doorway. He was brewing a pot of coffee. Emma was asleep in my bed, not stirring when either of us left the room. I'd slipped on my pants, but that was all. Ian was dressed, even had his gun belt slung low on his hips. It was late, close to midnight, and we had the house to ourselves. The only sound came from the ticking of the grandfather clock in the other room.

"Mason." Ian's hair was mussed and instead of going to sleep beside Emma, he'd be heading toward Bozeman to find out who had come for him.

"Evers won't come himself."

"Nay. A scouting party." He grabbed a mug. "He won't sully his hands with the dirty work."

I agreed. "The distance is too great, the time too long to be away. How can he justify a trip to America? The Duke of Everleigh going to America." I shook my head. "Wouldn't happen."

"We should be gone a week." He shrugged, took a sip of the hot brew, winced. The man made coffee as thick as mud in the springtime. "Evers' men can wait a day. They've waited five years. One more day willna make a difference, ye ken. I want – hell, need – to take care of Emma's step-brother first."

My ire for the man flared to life like embers on a fire. "Thomas James."

Ian nodded. "Aye. I'll take care of the bastard."

Through gritted teeth, I replied, "Good."

"You'll protect her?" With the change in topic, he turned his head to look at me. His eyes were...bleak.

"Of course. You take care of her step-brother, I'll watch over her."

"I hadn't expected this to happen so quickly. I kent Evers would come after me eventually, but right after we found Emma? A cruel twist of fate. We've only just made her ours. I should be here with you both, as she should be trained by both her men. This fuck-all situation is preventing this."

We learned more in Mohamir than defending the Crown. When we were in charge of protecting a local secular leader – a man with three brothers, all of whom shared a wife. We discovered the staid Victorian ways we'd been raised with were only for the man's gain. In England, a woman was a husband's property, to use and abuse as he saw fit, all the while fucking a string of mistresses, leaving his wife cold and unfulfilled. The Mohamiran leader's wife, when we met her, was a submissive in the five-person marriage, but was quite happy. She was cherished – a word the leader used frequently – and protected by not one man, but several. Her needs were met, every carnal desire fulfilled. When one of the brothers had died in a fall from a horse, she was not left alone, destitute and without a means to support herself or her children. We learned much from the leader, from all of the brothers, and we chose to follow the Mohamiran culture's claiming of a bride.

England was not the place to fulfill this alternative way of life. It would be too hard to hide. America, especially the West, was a new frontier, where open land abounded and men were free.

Ian and I had been close like brothers for years. There had been no question we would share a bride. Until Emma, the woman was just a dream. And now, she was upstairs, sleeping off our attentions. No way in bloody hell would Ian miss out on her. Evers wouldn't take that away from him as he had his rank, his military career and his country.

"Go. Take care of the problem, then come back."

"Her arse is mine, Kane." He looked at me directly. Clearly.

I nodded. "I'll get her ready for you."

I'd taken her virginity, her maidenhead. He would claim her arse.

"I'll be back."

EMMA

It was the second morning I awoke engulfed in a man's embrace. This one, however, was not Ian. I'd come to recognize my men quickly – had it only been two days? – and they felt differently, smelled differently, held me differently.

This was Kane. His hands were rougher. His scent was...him. Woodsy, fresh air. Cinnamon. Ian held me like two spoons in a drawer. Kane had me sprawled across the top of him, one of my legs tossed over his, my breasts pressed into him, the sprinkling of dark hair on his chest tickling me. I was comfortably settled with my head on his shoulder, my nose nudging his neck. I breathed him in, relishing his stillness. I could take my time to study him, think about him, what he and Ian had done to me the night before. The last I remembered, I was on my belly, my knees tucked beneath me, both men's hands between my spread thighs. They'd worked both my holes and I came, again and again. I'd been mindless, lost to the pleasure they'd wrung from my body. I hadn't cared that two men were touching me. I hadn't cared that Ian's fingers had penetrated my bottom. I hadn't cared that I'd sucked both men's cocks and swallowed all of their seed. They'd made it seem intimate and special and that my body was made just for them.

For, it seemed, it was. All of my senses awakened when I was with them. The depth of feeling was unlike I'd ever known before. My skin was more sensitive, my body more responsive. I felt delicious and wanton and delicate and brave. The last was more coerced than the others, but nonetheless, Ian and Kane made me *feel.* I had no idea what had been lacking in my life until now. It was early days yet, but I was ever so thankful that Thomas was such a terrible man and chose to leave me at the brothel. If not, I'd still be alone and bored tending to his children and assisting in quilt making and church lunches completely unaware of the bond between a woman and her husbands.

In the safe confine of Kane's arms, I assessed my body. I was sated, relaxed but there was something in my bottom, something hard and it filled me up. Clenching down, I tried to force it out, but it wouldn't budge. It had to be the plug they'd used yesterday before dinner, but put it in me once again after I fell asleep. It wasn't exactly uncomfortable, but it was...there.

His dark chest hair was right there to touch. I hadn't had a chance to lay with him when we were awake. The man was all action and authority. Now, with him asleep, I could feel his heart beating beneath my cheek, watch the rise and fall of his chest. The soft springy hair on his chest tickled and I carefully ran a finger through it. His skin was remarkably soft for someone so strong.

"I can hear you thinking," Kane murmured, his voice rough with sleep.

I stiffened in his arms, but when he squeezed me reassuringly, I relaxed. "I don't remember what happened last night."

"We made you come. Over and over."

I idly swirled my finger in his dark hair. "I remember that."

"Your body was too exhausted from all the pleasure to remain awake."

"Why?"

"Why did you come several times? Because you gave up your inhibitions, at least for a short duration. I assume they are back in full force now."

"Why do believe that to be true?" I asked, although I knew he was right, but I wasn't going to say so.

"Because you realize there's a plug in your arse."

"Yes, that," I grumbled.

He shifted and slid out from beneath me so I lay on my stomach.

"No, don't move," he said, coming up to kneel beside me. I looked over my shoulder and could see his cock, thrusting out fully erect from a thatch of dark hair. I'd taken it into my mouth! It had fit within me...and I'd liked it.

"Tuck your knees under you."

I frowned up at him. He just frowned back, so I complied. There was no question what he could see of me this way.

"Good girl. Unlike Ann, I think it's best for you to have your plug training solely while you sleep. Relax, I'm going to take it out."

I relaxed, perhaps because his hand was on my lower back as he worked the plug from my ass, or because I wouldn't have one filling me during the day. Wincing, I breathed out through my mouth as he gently tugged it free.

Once it was gone, I felt...empty.

"So pretty, baby." A finger ran over the stretched opening and I startled. "Shhh, easy. That worked so well. Tonight we'll try the bigger size."

He bent his body over mine so I felt the smattering of hair on his chest tickle my back. He whispered in my ear. "Did Ian tell you we'd fuck you every morning?"

I nodded, my pussy clenching, anticipating his cock. If he made me feel like they had last night, I was not going to complain.

"Good. Let's feel if you're ready." That's when I felt his fingers slip into me and there was no question I was eager for him. I sighed in pleasure and felt how easily his entrance was.

"Oh baby, you're so wet. Are you still sore?"

I shook my head. All I felt was delicious heat.

Shifting on his knees, I felt the thick head of his cock nudge my opening when he slipped his fingers free.

"You'll take me like this – from behind?" I asked, surprised as he filled me completely. I groaned.

"Oh, baby. Just like this."

CHAPTER NINE

EMMA

Breakfast was much like the evening meal with everyone eating around the large dining table. Ann was smiling at her husbands and did not seem in trouble or embarrassed by what had occurred the previous night, nor did she shimmy or shift in her seat.

"Thank you for letting me borrow some of your clothes," I told her as I sat down, Kane holding out the chair for me.

Ann smiled. "That dress looks lovely on you, although you seem to fill it out a bit better than I." The bodice *was* quite snug but Kane did not seem to mind as his eyes kept drifting down to the strained buttons.

Kane leaned down and whispered. "I rather like the dress as it is. Perhaps a few of these will pop off?" His finger flicked over the top button.

I rolled my eyes and grinned at him knowing how much he liked my breasts.

Once seated, the platters of eggs and ham being passed to me, did I realize we had some empty places. "Where's Ian? And, um...Mason?"

Sitting next to me, Kane took the platter of ham and put a

slice on my plate, then another on his. "He's gone to Bozeman."

Gone? I paused. "I thought he had work or chores to do. He left because of what you said last night?" I looked to Simon.

The man nodded.

"Why?" I asked.

Everyone glanced at Kane. Perhaps, as my husband, he was to answer. "I told you some of us were regimented together in Mohamir under the command of a man named Evers. An incident occurred and Ian was implicated. He was innocent, but framed."

"Framed?" I asked, worried for Ian. "For what?"

"Killing a number of women and children."

I sat wide-eyed at Kane's words. Ian wouldn't kill women and children. I hadn't known him long, but could vouch for his character nonetheless.

"Yes, what Brody said is true. Evers killed a family. I won't go into detail of why or how as it is too gruesome to share."

I put my fork down, my food having lost any appeal.

"When word spread of the horror, Evers pinned the crime on Ian."

I frowned. "Why would he do that?"

"He's a Scot, not English."

"So?"

"You are not familiar with English history," Andrew said in his American accent. "Neither was I until I met up with this group." He tilted his head indicating the Englishmen around the table.

"The Scots have wanted their freedom from the English for hundreds of years. The Battle of Culloden in the past century finished off the clans, but hatred still runs through the veins of men on both sides. Returning to England, Ian could be tried and convicted for Evers' crime for being a Scot alone; the hatred is that strong."

Panic flared. "We must go to him. Keep this man from taking Ian!" I pushed back my chair, yet Kane's hand on the high back halted me.

"Emma, stop." Kane's voice was deep and clear.

I shook my head furiously. "No, we need to help him."

He lowered his head so his dark eyes met and held mine. "I do not wish to spank you for disobedience when you are clearly thinking of Ian's best interest."

"But–" He put a finger over my lip, his brows raised.

"Do you think I, or any of these men, would sit here eating breakfast if we truly thought Ian was in danger?"

When he put it that way, I saw that I was acting rashly.

I let my shoulders slump in a very unladylike way. "It's just that...."

Kane kissed my brow, his lips warm. "I know."

Did he really know how much Ian was coming to mean to me? In such a short time, I cared for the man. Love? Perhaps not, but I didn't want to see him come to harm. He'd only treated me with the utmost of care. Tender, even. The idea of someone using him falsely, and in such a cruel, ruthless way left a bitter taste in my mouth.

"Does Evers have this much power?" I asked, needing the details. "He was stationed in Mohamir, a small country far from home. I beg your pardon, but that must not have been the most plum position."

I glanced between the men, a little fearful I spoke out of turn.

"We found it quite enlightening, until this event," Kane took my hand in his, reassuring me my words were not taken more deeply than deserved. "As you are well aware, being married to several men is not a Western custom."

"This man Evers has come all the way here to take Ian back to England?" The idea made the breakfast unappealing.

He squeezed my hand. "Evers wouldn't come here. He's too important in England, or at least he thinks that of himself. Besides, it's half a world away. We chose this location well. Once we learned of Evers' intentions to implicate Ian for his crimes, we banded together and departed Mohamir and worked our way here. To remain safe and keep Evers' secret."

"Here, we found a place to settle, to begin lives like the families in Mohamir," Simon added.

"A woman with several husbands," I finished.

"It's not something I was raised for," Ann told me and she looked to Robert, then Andrew. "But my straits were dire and I had to marry. Robert promised he would take care of me, to protect me and ensured I would never see my father again. He was a...cruel man."

A look of old pain crossed her face.

"I wanted her the moment I saw her," Robert said, lifting Ann's hand and kissing the knuckles, which made her brighten remarkably.

"It was quite a surprise when I learned that Andrew claimed me as his wife as well. It was...complicated." She chuckled and the other man smiled. They were clearly happy now, infatuated even and I remembered how they'd taken her together, all of them verbose in their pleasure.

"What are we to do, sit by idly while we wait for their return?" I asked, feeling helpless.

"There are no idle hands here on the ranch," Simon said, returning from the kitchen with a platter refilled with ham. "We work for the common good. We rotate turns cooking and tending to dishes as you saw last night. It is my task this morning. There is ample to do. Horses, cattle, fences, building maintenance, the list is never ending."

"What do you think would interest you, baby?" Kane asked.

I thought for a moment. I'd grown up with a cook, a housekeeper and other people to take care of the more mundane tasks. I was...had been a society woman and was not adept at ranch life.

"I can ride. Perhaps I can offer assistance in the stables?" I looked to Kane, then at the other men around the table.

"Then we shall begin the day there."

***

"Relax, Emma," Kane said in soothing tones. I was on my stomach, knees tucked under me in the usual position for having the plug put in or taken out. It was morning, so the latest plug had been in all night.

"I...I'm sorry," I replied, taking a deep breath, although it did nothing to settle me.

"You've only been awake a minute. What can you be so tense about?" He'd moved his hands from between my thighs and ran one up and down my back.

I sighed into my pillow. "Ian. I worry about Ian."

His hand continued it's slow, soothing motion. "Baby, there's no reason to worry. He's fine."

I looked over my shoulder at him, once again in awe. His shoulders were broad, his chest solid and with dark hair that tapered in a line below his navel to the thatch of hair at the base of his cock. His cock was always erect; there wasn't a time when I saw it at rest, even after a good fucking. Unruly locks of hair fell over his forehead. Sleep had softened his features, if that were even really possible. I was...enthralled.

"It's been five days," I pouted. I missed Ian. I had to admit to myself that I wanted both men. I wanted Kane...and Ian. It seemed like something – someone – was missing with Ian gone.

"I thought all the time with the horses would have distracted you."

I shook my head dejectedly. "I've enjoyed it, especially riding astride instead of sidesaddle. That seems so paltry though in comparison to what Ian's challenges."

His hand slid down my back to cup my bottom. "Take a deep breath and push out. That's it. Good girl." He slipped the plug from me and didn't delay working me with his fingers. This had been the routine in the days since Ian left. "You've done so well. I can now fit two fingers in you."

I breathed heavily from his ministrations; his two fingers – very large fingers – scissored and stretched my ass even more than the plug. The feeling wasn't something I would ever become used to. It was foreign and uncomfortable, yet the sensations elicited as his fingers brushed against the ring of muscle there had me panting and even coming. I disliked it, but loved it all the same.

"Ian will be so pleased when he returns. He will want to see your progress, to see you taking the progressively larger plugs. You will be ready for his cock. Why will he be pleased, baby?"

I moaned as he pushed the fingers in deep, the greasy lubricant from the plug still kept me slippery. "Because...because he will fuck me there."

"That's right. He's going to claim your virgin arse. After, we'll both fuck you. Together. Ian will fuck your arse while I fuck your tight cunny. What will that mean?"

He'd said these words to me every morning as he worked my body. It was a daily reminder as to Ian's inclusion in our marriage, that we would not be complete until he returned. That he was training my ass for Ian.

"That we are one."

Kane moved behind me and nudged the head of his cock at the entrance to my pussy. It was so broad, so flared that every time he filled me, he opened me so wide. "It will be like this, only better. My fingers are most certainly a poor substitute for Ian's big cock."

With those words, he thrust deep, filling my pussy, his fingers in my ass, coaxing me into complete submission. Kane was correct. With Ian missing, I came, but the pleasure I knew would not be the same until he returned and his cock was deep within me as well.

***

One challenge of ranch life I discovered was the lack of solitude. Kane remained close to me at night from dinner until breakfast. After eating in the morning, he went off to do whatever needed to be accomplished that day. Repairing a well, a breeding of a mare to the very eager stallion, stringing barbed wire, going into town for supplies. The list was never ending. When Kane was not about, I usually worked in companionship with at least one other man in the stable, if not more. Ann enjoyed working the garden, the immense patch of land that held all kinds of vegetables and fruit that would sustain our larder for the winter.

Today, however, the men were off working far afield and I was alone in the stable. I'd ridden each day, with the promise to remain in sight of the buildings when alone for my own safety. Fortunately, I'd done nothing to warrant a punishment from Kane while Ian had been away, which only helped me to settle into my daily tasks.

After saddling the horse Kane had chosen for me, I led the animal out of the stable and into the bright sunshine. The air was warm and fresh; a rain shower overnight left everything verdant.

I was just pulling a carrot I'd stolen from the kitchen out of my pocket to give to the animal when something in the distance caught my eye. It was a group of men, four of them, on horseback, although who they were was unclear. They were on a rise to the south, in the opposite direction of town.

A bad feeling settled in my stomach, knowing none of the men on the ranch had gone that way. Kane was with Brody and Simon tending to a sick calf in the north pasture. Rhys and Cross were stringing barbed wire to a repaired fence to the west. Ann was most likely in the garden at this hour.

Slowly, they came closer, their horses plodding over the terrain as if they had all the time in the world. Recognition was swift, even from such a distance, for I knew Ian's bearing, the breadth of his shoulders. He was with three other men. Strangers. Oh, dear lord.

Dropping the horse's lead, I sprinted into the stable to grab the rifle, locked and loaded, perched upon pegs in the wall, ready for use at any sign of danger. Kane had pointed it out to me the first day, ensuring I knew not only the dangers that abounded, but also how we protected ourselves from them.

I was surely familiar with a rifle. Before my parents died, my father had instructed me to shoot until I was competent in using one. He'd also provided a lifestyle that did not require doing so. Until now.

Returning to the horse, I mounted carefully with the loaded weapon and a long skirt and nudged my heels into his sides.

"Ann!" I shouted as I came upon the garden, dirt kicking up around me in a soft swirl.

She stood from her crouch by the summer raspberries.

"Ian is on the rise with several men."

Her eyes widened beneath the brim of her sun hat, from my words and most likely from the gun I had slung across my body. "Surely you aren't going to meet them?"

"He is with the men who sought him. I know it."

"How do you know such a thing?" she asked, her head turned in the direction of the rise, her hand on her forehead to block the sun.

I shook my head. "I just do." My heart raced and I was breathing as if I'd run the distance to the garden instead of riding.

"You can't mean to approach them yourself!" A look akin to horror crossed her face.

"What if they are here for the others?" I looked in the opposite direction to see if any of the men could be seen. "Do you want them all to be taken? Killed?"

"*You* could get killed," she countered, pointing at me.

"I have the rifle."

"Emma!" she shouted, but I'd already spurred my horse into a full gallop.

My bonnet slipped off my head from the brisk pace, bouncing against my back as it dangled from the ribbon about my neck. Ian was back and he was in danger.

When the men saw me approach, they stopped. I slowed to a trot, shifting the rifle so I could aim and fire at will.

Ian was indeed one of the men, Mason, I now recognized, on his left, two strangers on his right. They all appeared travel worn, with dusty clothes, skin tanned from the sun. The length of the scruff on their cheeks indicated several days in the saddle. To my eyes, Ian looked heavenly. He was whole and appeared uninjured. The look on his face, however, indicated his situation to be dire.

"You're not welcome here. Let Ian go and I won't shoot you," I warned.

The other men stared at me with mixed looks – amusement, anger and surprise. None held weapons as I did, however rifle butts protruded from two of the packs. They sat relaxed in their saddles, hands resting on the pommels.

"Would the lass shoot us?" one man asked Ian. His accent matched Ian's brogue.

My husband hadn't taken his eyes from me, although they narrowed at the question.

"I dinna ken," he replied. "Emma, put the gun down."

"No," I replied, shaking my head. "I won't let these men

take you back to England." I lifted the rifle so it pointed at the man on the far right. His hands came up slowly, and so did his eyebrows.

"I assume this is your wife," the man commented.

"Aye," Ian replied, his voice in that stern, low octave. "Emma, put the gun down." His repeated words were more insistent.

"We aren't taking your husband to England," the other stranger said. I shifted the gun his way.

"They're not, Emma," Mason added.

"How do I know you aren't lying?" My palms were damp and my shoulders began to ache from holding up the heavy rifle, but I held true.

"Because I said so," Ian said. He nudged his horse forward until he came along side me and grabbed the weapon from my hands. I exhaled at the relief of Ian taking charge and so did the other three men. "So did Mason."

Up close, a tick pulsed in his jaw, his eyes narrowed not in lust as I so wanted to see from him, but in anger. "Are ye daft?" he asked, his voice loud. "Waving a gun around, approaching men ye dinna ken?"

His Scot's brogue was stronger than usual.

"You're innocent," I affirmed.

"He is," a man behind him said.

I paused at the words, looked to Ian for confirmation.

"These men are MacDonald and McPherson. Scots like me. They were part of our regiment in Mohamir and have come to join us. They have surnames, but they've never shared them."

I looked around Ian and to the men. They tipped their hats at me and I blushed. Mason just gave a subtle shake of his head as if he were in disbelief.

"Oh dear," I whispered, my shoulders slumping.

Ian turned and tossed the rifle to one of the other men, caught easily and readily in the way only those used to such weaponry did. My husband slid from his horse, came around and stood at my side, arms out. "Get down, Emma."

"Then why are they here?" I asked, ignoring his order.

He sighed, but did not dim his anger. "As I said, they've come to live here. They emigrated to America."

"What?" That was the last possible scenario I'd expected. Turning my head to the men briefly, I saw the truth of the words with slight nods from each.

"MacDonald, the lug, is Simon's brother. Now get down from the bloody horse."

Now that it was made apparent, the resemblance was clear. Oh dear. I was in dire straits.

I looked down at Ian for the briefest of moments, knew from the look in his eye, the set of his jaw, the timbre of his voice that I was in the worst kind of trouble. Tossing one leg over the saddle, I let Ian lower me to the ground, take my hand and drag me several feet away to a large boulder, one of many that dotted the rugged landscape. He sat and abruptly pulled me over his knees, my belly down.

"Ian!" I shouted, right before the air escaped my lungs in a loud oomph. I'd expected him to pull me into a hug, a kiss, something to end the drought of attention and affection his days away had brought.

Unceremoniously, he hoisted my skirt up and over my back, exposing my naked ass to the air, Ian and the three men. He did not talk, did not delay, only spanked me – hard – all over my ass so that the flesh there and on the upper part of my thighs prickled with heat.

"Ye will nay approach danger with complete disregard."

Smack.

"Ye came alone."

Smack.

"Wielding a gun that could have been taken from ye and used on your person without effort."

Smack.

"Did ye ken Mason and I that weak that we couldn't protect ourselves against two men?"

Smack.

"Where the bloody hell is Kane?"

Smack. Smack. Smack.

I started to cry, my hands gripping the tall blades of summer grass. The searing strikes had me wilted and contrite. I *had* ridden into presumed danger without a care to my safety. I *had* aimed a gun toward men who had outnumbered me and could have overpowered me readily enough. I'd been headstrong and desperate.

"They were going to take you away!" I shouted, then sniffled.

"She's a little hellcat, lad." The voice came from behind me. Oh, the men! I forgot they were there and most assuredly watching my punishment.

"I'd like a little lassie to defend me like that." Another man's voice broke through the sound of Ian's palm striking my already tender flesh.

"You would, but then you'd spank her arse just like Ian."

Tears ran down my cheeks as Ian continued, my humiliation complete not only from these strangers commenting on my misery as if it were nothing, but by the sound of horses approaching and knowing the men from the ranch would see me this way as well.

I heard the men talking, but couldn't hear the words, dipping into a place where the spanking had switched from painful to a fog, although each strike was still filled with vehemence. I had succumbed. I was out of control, at the mercy of Ian and his palm, his anger, his fear. Wait. His anger was because of his fear for me. His punishment was to ensure that I was whole and hale, but also to soothe his frazzled nerves that I could have been harmed if I had approached more nefarious men.

"Are you finished?"

Kane.

"Aye."

"Good. It's my turn."

The spanking began once again in earnest, this time it was Kane's palm, although he only added about five swats to the tally.

My world upended and I dizzily landed on Ian's hard thighs. I hissed out a breath at the contact. Using my hands, I wiped the streaks of tears from my cheeks as I sniffled. "I'm...I'm sorry," I mumbled, still recovering.

Kane knelt down beside me. "You scared ten years off my life when Ann told us where you'd gone."

"Are you going to spank me again?" I asked, glancing between both men. They looked at me with a mixture of fear and anger. Kane was breathing hard and sweat dotted his brow.

"Nay," Ian said. "I'm going to fuck you." I felt the truth of his words hard beneath my bottom.

"Now? Here?" There were the two strangers who who'd arrived with Ian, plus Mason. From the ranch were Brody, Simon and Cross. Simon and his brother were hugging and smacking each other on the back congenially, clearly pleased to be in each other's company after so many years.

"Now. Here," Ian repeated, shifting me on his lap so I still sat astride his thighs, but this time with my knees on either side of his hips. Kane grabbed the tangle of my dress and pulled it up around my waist and out of the way. Reaching between us, Ian undid the placket of his pants, his engorged cock bobbing free. Without a chance to even consider what we were about to do, he hoisted me up by my waist and lowered me directly onto his cock, filling my pussy in one smooth slide.

"Oh!" I cried out, feeling so full and surprised by how wet I was for him. I wanted to lift and lower myself on him, to use his cock to seek my pleasure, but he wouldn't let me. His hands, banded tightly about my waist, held me in place as he shifted his hips, thrusting up into me, using me.

"No! The men are watching," I pushed on his shoulders, frantic to rise. The feel of him inside of me was...delicious, but I did not wish to be watched, exposed as we were. "It's...it's private!"

"Stop, baby." Kane's voice cut through my panic. "The men, they're gone." Gripping tightly to Ian's shirt, I turned my head and saw the backs of the retreating men upon their horses. "This is not a theater show. Your punishment was warranted for your reckless behavior and they observed it, knowing now you are contrite and will not put your life, or those of anyone else, in danger. But fucking, they did not need to see."

I relaxed every tense muscle, which had me sinking lower on Ian's cock. He nudged the very entrance to my womb and I moaned.

"Ye are nay to come, Emma." Ian took me hard, filling me roughly. My breath escaped with every thrust. "Open her dress. I want to see her breasts."

Kane stepped behind me, reached around and ripped my bodice open, little buttons flying through the air. Dipping his hands into my corset, Kane lifted my breasts free.

"Oh, look at ye. I love the sight of ye getting well fucked," Kane said in my ear.

I cried out from one adept stroke.

"You're so beautiful. Can you feel how much Ian wants you? How much he's missed you? How desperate he was when you wanted to rescue him?"

My breasts jiggled with each hard slap of my thighs against his. The sound of my arousal, slippery wet and slick, filled the air.

"Dinna come, Emma," Kane warned.

My head fell back, my eyes squeezed shut as I panted. "Why?" Ian sucked a nipple into his mouth, drew on it, tugging the tip into a tight furl.

"Ye must ken how frantic I felt when you charged up the hillside," Ian growled against my breast. His short beard was soft and prickly at the same time, only heightening my sensitivity. "How desperate I was. So out of control. It is nay your job to rescue me. It is your job to remain safe or you will make me insane."

His hands tightened about my waist just as he pulled me down onto him, his cock swelling inside of me as he came, his hot seed coating my womb.

His sweaty forehead pressed against my breasts as he recovered, his breath soughing out of his lungs, but he loosened his secure hold. Not that I had any intention of moving. I had his cock filling me up and I wanted completion only he could give me. Clenching my inner walls around him, I felt tremors of my desire, but it wasn't enough to make me come. It seemed it was not to happen. Even shifting my hips offered no relief.

"Is she ready?" Ian asked, his hot breath fanning my chest.

"Yes," Kane replied.

He lifted his head and looked at me. Desire was still etched in the hard line of his jaw, his pale eyes hooded from his release. "Your arse is ready for me, Emma?"

I clenched his cock once again, the idea of him taking me as they'd planned, now, had my arousal simmering. I was so desperate, so needy for my release, Ian's cock buried within me while remaining still was torture. "Yes." I repeated Kane's words.

Ian plucked at a long tendril of my hair.

"Then it is time."

CHAPTER TEN

IAN

I scrubbed the dirt and sweat from hard days on a horse. The water in the hip tub was cold, but it didna matter. Emma's cries of pleasure and begging wafted through the air from Kane's bedroom. After I'd recovered from fucking her – and the scare to my heart when I'd seen her galloping and gun wielding – I'd tossed her onto my lap for the ride back to the house. I hadn't been afraid for her safety as we wouldna hurt her, but knowing she would have done something so dangerous if I really had been in trouble had my ire rise. She had nay thought to her safety. She dinna ken what she meant to me.

Mason had been waiting to take care of the horses as Kane and I took care of our wife. Once upstairs, we stripped her bare and unceremoniously tied her hands to the brass headboard.

This hadn't been done without questions or opposition from Emma, who vehemently apologized and protested. She was not going to go off and do something dangerous like that again. While I bathed, Kane worked her body, keeping her arousal elevated, yet not allowing her to come. The spanking had been her punishment, rightly enough, but torturing her with pleasure was a perk I relished as I scrubbed my body clean.

When I'd come across MacDonald and McPherson in Bozeman, I'd expected a kill-or-be-killed situation. There was nay chance of my return to England. There was nay chance, if Evers had indeed tracked me down personally, he would have let me live to make such a journey. When I'd found my friends to be the men Simon had heard about, the relief had been immeasurable. Discovering they wished to live in the Montana Territory, start anew as well, only made me happy. I ken Simon must've felt the irony at discovering one of the men who he'd alerted me to was indeed his brother.

And so we returned as a merry group, until Emma rushed up the rise like Boadicea, all beauty and fierce protectiveness. This lack of personal safety proved to me that she considered me hers just as much as she was mine. The revelation had me grinning, sitting naked in a small tub with my knees practically by my ears. She hadn't said that she loved us, but her actions spoke for her. She would not have ridden into potential danger if she didna care. I felt at peace for the first time in...years. Evers was still a threat, but I could not live my life in constant fear of the man. I could, however, live the rest of my days with Emma with me, between me and Kane. I was possessive of her, perhaps excessively so, but that was what a husband felt for his woman. Protectiveness, possessiveness and the stirrings of love. I finished my bath with additional haste and returned to my family.

Kane had her legs spread, knees bent. His hand between her

thighs, two fingers filling her arse. From where I stood in the doorway, drying myself, I could see he was ensuring she was completely slick with the lubricant.

Emma was stunning. Her eyes were closed, her head back, mouth open. Chestnut locks fanned out on the pillow behind her head, her arms over her head with her wrists secured. This placement forced her breasts up, her nipples tight and a cherry red. Perhaps the moans I'd heard from the tub had been Kane playing with those sweet tips. There was additional length in the rope, but the knots securing her were sufficient. She was just where we wanted her.

Kane looked to me, his gaze hooded, his desire evident in the rigidity of his cock. At some point he'd stripped as well. "She's ready."

"Yes, please. Ian, I need to come!" Emma begged, her breathing ragged and deep.

Kane moved to lie next to Emma, side by side. I knelt on the bed, lifted Emma up and flipped her over so she was astride Kane's waist, one of her knees on either side of his hips. With her wrists tied, she couldna move. Kane slipped his head between her arms. As I reached for the jar of lubricant, Kane shifted Emma as he wanted, forcing her down onto his cock. My seed from her earlier fucking made the action easy and both of them made sounds of pleasure.

Coating my fingers, I tested her tight pink pucker. It had

been days since I'd touched her here, but Kane had assured me of her readiness. I took a moment to play, circling my fingers over the slick opening, pushing against the tight ring. When my fingers slipped in without much effort, I knew he was correct. The feel of her, so tight with Kane's cock right there, separated from my fingers with just a thin membrane, had my balls tightening and the need to claim her intense.

"Oh God," Emma moaned.

"It's time, baby. Time to make you ours. Together."

"Yes!" she cried as Kane rocked his hips up into her.

Coating my cock with additional lubricant, I nudged the broad head to her virgin hole. I took her only a short time ago, but my cock was pulsing, aching to feel her walls around it once again. Carefully, slowly, I pressed forward, knowing my cock was larger than any of the plugs Kane had used on her while I'd been away. She might have adjusted to accept something filling her, but a cock was different. Bigger, deeper and most certainly harder.

Stroking a hand down her back, soothing her, I murmured words of encouragement. *Good girl. You're ours now. Ah, my cock's in you. Relax. You took another inch. Such a pretty sight taking both our cocks. Breathe, baby. That's it. I'm in all the way.*

She was completely filled. Little mewling sounds escaped her throat as she held perfectly still. I met Kane's gaze. His jaw was clamped tightly, undoubtedly struggling to hold off pumping into her just as I was. We both took a moment to let her settle, let her adjust to having us cram her so bloody full. Her back was so silky smooth against the hard line of my chest. Kane lifted his hands to cup her breasts, rub his thumbs over her sensitive tips. With her hands bound, she could do nothing but accept whatever we gave her.

"You're so big. I'm filled so deep. I...I don't know what to do," she whimpered. Her pale skin was coated in a sheen of perspiration, her hair clinging to her damp skin. She licked her lips, her eyes closed.

"You don't have to do anything, baby. It's time for us to take care of you," Kane said. He offered me a brief nod and he moved, pulled back so he almost withdrew, then slid back in. As he did so, I pulled back, so we worked in opposition, one filling her as the other retreated. We kept a slow pace, a consistent, mind-numbing pace. "This is where you belong. Between us. You were made to be filled by our cocks. You're ours, baby."

"Ours," I repeated on a growl.

Emma was lost, wild, abandoned. She cried out, tears sliding down her cheeks as she pushed her breasts into Kane's palms. We didn't stop, didn't let her catch her breath. "Yes!"

"Come, baby. Your pleasure belongs to us. *You* belong to us."

At my command, she came, screaming so loud the men in

the stable had to have heard. Her body squeezed and pulsed around my cock, which had me falling off the cliff directly after her. I couldn't hold back with the tight constriction of her arse. My seed filled her up. Kane followed directly after, pulling her down onto his chest, letting her recover as we were connected as one.

EMMA

I must have dozed, for when I came awake, I was curled into Kane's side, Ian pressed against my back, my body feeling empty as their cocks were gone. I did, however, feel the remnants of their releases, sticky and warm coating my pussy and thighs. My hands had been released. The room was bright with daylight, only just shy of the noon meal. We were in bed, lounging during a busy summer's day on the ranch. It felt...decadent. I reveled in the feel of both men surrounding me.

Ian was home. He was safe.

Kane kissed my forehead as I felt Ian's hand stroking my back.

"Ye willna go off trying to save me again, Emma," Ian said, just before kissing my spine.

"We are here to protect you. There are two of us, yet only one of you," Kane added.

"But you are irreplaceable!" Didn't they understand that I wanted both of them?

"Ah, lass," Ian breathed. "It's our job to protect ye. To possess ye just like we did."

"I can feel your possessiveness dripping out of me," I replied dryly.

"Mmm, yes. It's a beautiful sight."

I idly swirled my finger through the soft hairs on Kane's chest. "If your job is to protect me, what is my job?"

Kane retreated and turned me so I was on my back between them. He delved his hand between my thighs and through their mixed seed. I looked into his dark eyes. All hints of anger, of lust, were gone. In its place was most definitely the possessiveness he spoke of. "To take our seed. Again and again until it takes root and you swell with our child."

Ian came up on an elbow on my other side and looked down at me. "Do ye ken this is enough to make a baby, lass? We are a family, and soon, hopefully very soon, a growing family. Nothing will separate us."

"Nothing," Kane reiterated.

"What of the others?"

Kane frowned. "You ask after the other men while Ian plays with your cunny?"

"They need to find their own wives," Ian muttered.

"Perhaps, Kane, we have not done enough to make her remember to whom she belongs."

He slipped a finger into me and I sighed. "I...I remember."

"I'm not so sure," Kane countered. "Since it is your job to make the baby, it is most certainly your men's job to fill you with seed to do so."

"I...I would not want you to be remiss in your duties," I said, my eyes falling shut as my legs fell wide.

Ian moved between my legs and filled me in one easy stroke. "I will never get enough, lass."

His breath fanned my neck.

"Never," Kane added.

"Never," I whispered, as my husbands claimed me once again.

ABOUT THE AUTHOR

SIGN UP FOR VANESSA'S MAILING LIST FOR LATEST NEWS and get a FREE book!

http://freeeroticbook.com

USA Today Bestseller of steamy historical westerns

Who doesn't love the romance of the old West? Vanessa Vale takes the sensual appeal of rugged cowboys a step further with her bestselling books set in the Montana Territory. They are much more than just sexy historical westerns. They're deliciously naughty reads that sometimes push the boundaries of fantasy. It's pure escapism with quite a few very hot, very alpha cowboys.

When she's not writing, Vanessa savors the insanity of raising two boys, is figuring out how many meals she can make with a pressure cooker, and teaches a pretty mean karate class. She considers herself to be remarkably normal, exceedingly introverted and fairly vanilla, which does not explain her steamy stories and her fascination with cowboys, preferably more than one at a time. If that weren't enough, she also writes under the pen name, Vanessa Dare.

She lives in the Wild Wild West where there's an endless source of 'research' material.

Vanessa loves to hear from fans!

Please write and share a review you posted!

vanessavaleauthor@gmail.com

@iamvanessavale on Twitter

and on Facebook

OTHER BOOKS BY VANESSA VALE

Montana Maidens

Claiming Catherine

Taming Tessa

Dominating Devney

Submitting Sarah

Montana Men

The Lawman

The Cowboy

The Outlaw

Western Widows

Sweet Justice

Bridgewater Menage Series

Their Kidnapped Bride

Their Wayward Bride

Their Captivated Bride

Their Treasured Bride

Their Christmas Bride

Their Reluctant Bride

Wildflowers Of Montana

Rose

Hyacinth

Dahlia

Daisy

VANESSA DARE BOOKS

Relentless

Mine To Take

Naked Choke

CPSIA information can be obtained
at www.ICGtesting.com
Printed in the USA
LVOW04s1314200416
484499LV00002BB/397/P